Betrayal

Betrayal

Marquis de Sade

Translated by Andrew Brown

ET REMOTISSIMA PROPE

Hesperus Classics

Hesperus Classics
Published by Hesperus Press Limited
4 Rickett Street, London SW6 1RU
www.hesperuspress.com

First published by Hesperus Press Limited, 2006

Introduction and English language translation © Andrew Brown, 2006
Foreword © John Burnside, 2006

Designed and typeset by Fraser Muggeridge studio
Printed in Jordan by Jordan National Press

ISBN: 1-84391-136-1
ISBN13: 978-1-84391-136-4

CONTENTS

FOREWORD

The first time I read Sade I was reminded of my time studying Classics at an impoverished comprehensive school, where my ancient, dog-eared translation of *The Odyssey* had been carefully edited to conceal from my impressionable mind anything that might be considered salacious. Key scenes – for example, the episode in which the naked Odysseus is washed up on the beach where Nausicaa and her maidens are strolling – had been left in the original Greek, sending me off to the dictionary to find out what I was missing, just as early translations of Sade left certain passages in French, to ensure that impressionable Anglo-Saxon minds might not be corrupted by that foreign aristocrat's bizarre sexual imaginings. Violence, though often extreme, was faithfully rendered; sex was obfuscated. It made me think that Sade was *all about* sex, and that 'sadism' – the ritualisation of an exquisite sexual cruelty – was something that the 'Divine Marquis' had invented. Not till later, after close, and less feverish, readings, did I realise that Sade wasn't really interested in sex, per se, and that, though he may well have been the 'philosopher in the boudoir' he was reputed to be, it was philosophy, and not the boudoir, that obsessed him.

We ritualise what we most love and what we most fear (sometimes the two are identical). What Sade ritualises is power on the one hand and humiliation on the other; sex in his writings is usually rather unceremonious, devoid of sensuality, tenderness or erotic charge. Set any of his books beside *Venus in Furs*, or *L'Histoire d'O*, and it soon becomes obvious that Sade cares not a whit for the ceremonies of sex, or for the nuances of power play between dominant and submissive partners. Sade is all about force, or cunning persuasion; partnership, collusion, *play* hardly ever come into it. This is what makes him such a pessimist: he is an aristocrat, both by blood and by temperament and, for the aristocrat, negotiation is not permitted. At the same time, his obsession with power and humiliation makes him a perfect subject for feminist theory: he takes the most rigid patriarchal position to its logical conclusion and, in so doing, he builds a perfect *reductio ad absurdum*. Sex and violence really *are* two quite different things, but we have become so used to equating them in our most public fantasies that, ironically, we need a Sade to show us where we are going wrong.

An aristocrat of another kind once said that power is the ultimate aphrodisiac (presumably to explain why women were so attracted to *him*) – which suggests that using sex to create an illusion of power is to get things back to front. Of course, sex and power are close cousins, but the relationship only becomes interesting if one or the other is raised to the level of play. This is why flirting, for example, is so much more interesting than consummation. Play, however, is as far from Sade's mind as mutual pleasure: for him, power is a serious matter, which is why it is always predicated upon humiliation. In Sade, to lack power leads inevitably to abasement; by the same token, the powerful only seem capable of fulfilment through the humiliation of others. It's a poor view of the world, but a superb diagnosis of a certain class: a class that, according to Sade, included magistrates, the clergy, doctors and, worst of all, mothers-in-law.

In Michel Deville's witty, elegant 1988 film, *La Lectrice*, the much underappreciated actress Miou-Miou plays a professional reader, a beautiful, carefree young woman named Marie, whose unorthodox activities in a French provincial town provoke concern in high places. As the lives of Marie's clients are radically altered in response to her readings of

Baudelaire, Lewis Carroll and Marguerite Duras, among others, it becomes apparent that reading aloud is not quite the innocent pastime for which it was first mistaken and, faced with this instance of *l'imagination au pouvoir*, the powers that be decide that something must be done. After numerous attempts to scare Marie out of her vocation, they finally prepare a particularly nasty, if rather subtle, trap. This trap is sprung by a magistrate, a smug, condescending, venomous little man (beautifully played by Pierre Dux), who calls Marie to read to him, choosing as his preferred text a particularly explicit work by Sade. In the scene that follows, the good-natured but far from naive Marie finds herself outmanoeuvred, and has no choice but to retire, still in possession of her self-respect, having refused to play the magistrate's humiliating game.

It's a nice joke, that Marie's nemesis should come in the form of a Sade-loving magistrate, for the great satirist of misplaced power hated this class of official more than anyone else (with one exception). Innocent, in his own eyes, of any crime, Sade found himself executed in effigy, then imprisoned, first at Vincennes, and later in the Bastille, by court officials eager to do the bidding of his scandalised mother-in-law, Mme de Montreuil – that one exception for whom Sade reserved his purest, and most righteous, anger. Art being art, and his years in prison being long, he soon came up with a way of attacking both the despised magistrates and the mother-in-law who had dedicated her life to his destruction, in one gloriously scatological and biting satire. The real-life individual whom the 'Divine Marquis' chose as the butt of his tirade in *The Magistrate Mocked* was one de Fontein: in the text, he becomes Fontanis, or simply *le Président*, (the usual term for a magistrate). But it was his mother-in-law that Sade had most firmly in his sights, and the family nickname of that pious, hypocritical woman was, it seems, *la Presidente*. It must have pleased him, as he set about writing this most purely satirical of his works, that he was creating such a grotesque, loathsome – and masculine – portrait of the woman who had done so much to harm him, and whom he so thoroughly detested.

– *John Burnside, 2006*

INTRODUCTION

'Finished this story on 16th July 1787 at 10 p.m.,' noted Sade at the end of *The Magistrate Mocked.* He had then spent ten years more or less continuously behind bars, first in Vincennes (from which he managed to escape), then in the Bastille, where the *Magistrate* was composed. Two years after completing the story, on 2nd July 1789, he was to cause some alarm by shouting from the window of his cell to the crowds outside, 'They are murdering the prisoners!' Two days later he was transferred to the insane asylum at Charenton. Ten days after that, the Bastille fell.

By this time, he had begun to compose *The 120 Days of Sodom*, his most exhaustive catalogue of sexual activities: the loss of his manuscript, during his transferral from the Bastille to Charenton, filled him with despair, though he eventually managed to compose a new version. *The 120 Days*, whose title vies to outdo earlier feats of storytelling such as the *Decameron* (ten days) or the *Cent Nouvelles* (one hundred stories), is a work of relentless imaginative rigour, and is of all Sade's works the one that most deserves the epithet 'sadistic', even though the questions it raises (about sex, human identity, pleasure and pain, storytelling and enactment) far transcend the reductive connotations of that word. *The Magistrate Mocked* is a much shorter and lighter affair: a suburb of the Sadean city. It reveals an aspect of Sade that is less well known, as his usual mixture of hyper-refined language and brutal sexual fact is here replaced by something more knockabout and teasing. There is cruelty here, but it is not (as so often, most clearly in *Justine*) exercised against an innocent victim, but against a lawyer. Indeed, Sade's protagonist, M. de Fontanis, is set up as an object of scorn and derision for several reasons. Not only is he a lawyer; he is from Provence – and Sade's own Provençal origins do not stop him satirising the speech and manners of his fellow southerners repeatedly, especially since Fontanis finds himself among Parisians, and comments, ruefully, on how he had always known that these 'caustic and facetious' people would fail to treat him with the proper respect. Second, as a lawyer he is a professional man, a bourgeois, whose hubris in thinking he can marry into a family of nobles far above him in the social hierarchy of the *ancien régime* makes him ripe for a fall. Third, the object of the matrimonial ambitions of this cantankerous, pompous, and generally unappetising man of law (Sade's pen-portrait of him in the opening pages has a surrealistic savagery to it), Mlle de Téroze, is already in love with the young and dashing Count d'Elbène, giving rise to a situation not at all unlike that portrayed in the play *The Barber of Seville*, first performed in Paris in 1775 – though it is doubtful whether *The Magistrate Mocked* would be suitable material for a comic opera, even with music by Rossini: it is more of a *commedia dell'arte* piece, with some potential for film treatment (the scene with the balloon). Thus Fontanis is triply typecast as an object of satire: socially, sexually and professionally. The values of the Téroze and d'Olincourt families are barely mocked: the only hint of overt criticism lies in the fact that the Baron de Téroze is so foolish as to wish his daughter to wed a lawyer. It is the fact that the pompous wretch Fontanis *is* a lawyer that most arouses the text's indignation, and since the story alludes in the clearest of terms to specific (and unusual) events in Sade's own life, there is an autobiographical animus at work. As the story progresses, it becomes ever clearer that Sade is out to get at lawyers in particular because they offer the protection of the law to prostitutes who are at risk from their clients. (Sade's general view of prostitution seems to have been that it was a cash relationship, and he himself frequented the brothels of Paris in the 1760s, becoming such a notorious figure there that he got himself banned from several of them, no doubt for 'sadistic' practices.) The text, although to some extent in line with Sade's other work in its 'libertine' flavour (though it, no doubt ironically, rebukes Mlle de Téroze for having relinquished her virginity before marriage), breaks out into invective and indignation at the idea that prostitutes might be worth legal protection. There is a hint of Lear's denunciations of the legal profession in the way Sade's text angrily turns on Fontanis ('Thou rascal beadle, hold thy bloody hand!/Why dost thou lash that whore? Strip thine own back;/Thou hotly lust'st to use her in that kind/For which thou whipp'st her': one of the most 'sadistic' (or sado-masochistic) moments in all of Shakespeare, uniting sex, pain, and the law). Indeed, the text here becomes positively unbalanced: it loses its cool, sinking to illogicality (Fontanis is described as availing himself only moderately of the services of prostitutes, and having desires that go beyond his powers – and yet in one of the most disagreeable of the farcical tricks played on him, he manages to be 'crowned by love' five times in succession: not a bad tally) and resorting to diatribe (d'Olincourt acts as a mere mouthpiece for Sade's own attacks on the lawyers of Provence).

Through all the ranting, however, Sade's text does take up certain positions: for instance, in spite of Sade's own reputation for bloodthirsty violence, he voices his (unexpected) hostility to the death penalty, a hostility expressed in many other texts. Here, however, it is judicial violence of a particular kind that arouses his ire: the 'violence' of the law as exerted in defence of prostitutes, and against members of his own class – more specifically, as when the ghosts enumerate Fontanis's crimes, against Sade himself. At least one of the events included in the indictment against the magistrate (the one allotted to the year 1772) alludes quite closely to Sade's career, for in that year he was accused, with his manservant Latour, of having tried to poison four prostitutes in Marseilles. In fact he had 'merely' handed them out sweets laced with an excessive dose of the aphrodisiac Spanish Fly. Although the women all recovered, two of them brought charges of sodomy and attempted poisoning against Sade, who, together with Latour, was sentenced to death by (of course) the *parlement* of Aix-en-Provence; they fled and were duly executed in effigy (Sade's effigy was beheaded, Latour's hanged, as class distinctions dictated). Sade was eventually cleared of the charges. (It is perhaps noteworthy that prostitutes could actually have such charges against an aristocrat listened to seriously in the first place: yet another reason for Sade's haughty wrath.) The ghostly admonishment in the story in fact seems to conflate the *affaire de Marseille* with the earlier *affaire d'Arcueil*. On Easter Sunday, 1768, Sade met a young widow named Rose Keller in the street, and (as he later told the story) offered her money in exchange for sex. They went to his house in Arcueil, a suburb of Paris, where he inflicted a severe beating on her: their accounts as to whether Keller had consented, and the exact nature of the wounds caused, differed, but doctors who later examined her agreed that she had indeed been thrashed on the buttocks – a detail that we find entered in the ghosts' ledger for 1772, though here the excuse given is that the woman in question was a courtesan who had inflicted the protagonist with a venereal disease, and the punishment was merely 'playful'. Of course, all of these links with Sade's life are teasing and speculative, but the savage indignation of his text against the members of the legal profession on whom he blamed his persecution is not.

For all the anger, however, the story is ultimately a comedy, almost a bedroom farce with a heavy dose of scatological humour thrown in. The grim, programmatic exhaustiveness of *The 120 Days of Sodom* is missing, and the philosophising (for instance the appeals to 'nature') is relatively low-key and occasional. Its companion piece here, *Émilie de Tourville*, is much less amusing: again, its momentum is fuelled by indignation against a social order that places such a premium on women's premarital virginity, again the villains are associated with the law (one wicked brother is a lawyer, the other a councillor) and again it has autobiographical resonances: Sade's mother-in-law, Madame de Montreuil, pursued him relentlessly for besmirching the family 'honour', just as Émilie's brothers exact a chilling revenge on their sister for the same crime. *Émilie* is closer to Sade's 'gothic' style, with brooding forests, solitary incarceration, a suffering (and relatively innocent) woman, and general grimness. *The Magistrate Mocked* includes a few gothic elements too (the haunted chateau), but only in the service of the comedy. It is more sociable and oddly humane than many of Sade's other works, being almost Molièresque at times (for Molière's plays also mocked bourgeois pretensions to an aristocratic marriage, elderly men who claim a young and beautiful bride, people who speak in funny accents, and, of course, lawyers). And yet its deeper theme is a serious one. Are the human, all-too-human executors of the law adequate to their calling? Are human laws as they stand unjust, needing to be revised, perhaps by a 'philosophically' minded elite ('enlightened' aristocrats such as Sade, perhaps)? Finally, why the title *Betrayal*? (Apart from *traduttore traditore*, of course.) Because of the many small betrayals in the two stories: women betray their families by yielding to the temptations of premarital sex, and are betrayed in turn by fathers and brothers who impose unsuitable husbands or spectacular retribution on them; lawyers betray their calling; trust in one's hosts, rescuers and lovers is betrayed at every turn. And because of the one great betrayal that Sade here hints at: the betrayal of nature by the laws that human beings, perhaps illegitimately, perhaps perfectly naturally, impose on her.

– Andrew Brown, 2006

Note on the text:
The text I have used is that in *Historiettes, contes et fabliaux* in the *Oeuvres complètes* of the Marquis de Sade, edited by Annie Le Brun and Jean-Jacques Pauvert, vol. 3 (Paris: Pauvert, 1986). *The Magistrate Mocked* was originally *Le Président Mystifié*, where the epithet implies 'hoaxed' – someone against whom a *mystification* or practical joke has been played.

Betrayal

The Magistrate Mocked

For you can take my word: these people I will so
Depict that they will never more their faces show.

It was with the most intense regret that the Marquis d'Olincourt, a colonel in the dragoons, a man of wit, grace and vivacity, saw Mlle de Téroze, his sister-in-law, consigned to the embrace of one of the most dreadful mortals who have ever walked the face of the earth. That lovely girl, eighteen years of age, as fresh as Flora and as beautiful as the Graces,[1] had been loved for four years by the young Count d'Elbène, a lieutenant-colonel in d'Olincourt's regiment; she too could not repress a shudder as she saw the approach of the fateful moment that would, in joining her to the cantankerous husband who had been chosen for her, separate her forever from the only man worthy of her: but how could she prevent it? Mademoiselle de Téroze had an old, obstinate father, hypochondriac and gouty, who sadly imagined that it was neither the personality nor the qualities of a potential husband that should determine a girl's feelings for him, but only his good sense, maturity of age and, in particular, social rank. Now the status enjoyed by a man of law was the most esteemed and most majestic of all social ranks under a monarchy, and in any case this was the class of man that he loved best in all the world; only with a man of law could his younger daughter ever be really happy. However, the old Baron de Téroze had given his first daughter to a soldier, and, what is worse, to a colonel of dragoons; this girl, a very happy person and one who in every way seemed born for happiness, had no reason to regret her father's choice. But none of this made any difference; while this first marriage had succeeded, this was merely a piece of good luck; in fact, only a man of law could make a girl *really* happy; given this fact, it had become necessary to find a lawyer: now of all possible lawyers, the most agreeable in the eyes of the old Baron was a certain M. de Fontanis, President of the *Parlement* of Aix,[2] whom he had known previously in Provence. And so, without his sparing the matter a thought, it was decided that M. de Fontanis was to become the husband of Mlle de Téroze.

Not many people can imagine a president of the *Parlement* of Aix – it is a species of beast of which people have often spoken without knowing it well: strict and unbending by profession, and pernickety, credulous, stubborn, vain, cowardly, garrulous and stupid by character; with a beaky little face, rolling his 'r's like a Punchinello,[3] commonly as thin as a rake, lanky and skinny and stinking like a corpse… It seems that all the spleen and haughtiness of all the magistrates in the kingdom has taken refuge in this temple of the Themis of Provence,[4] to gush out as and when needed, each time that a French court has remonstrances[5] to bring or citizens to hang. But M. de Fontanis was even worse than this rapid sketch of his compatriots would suggest. Over the gaunt, and indeed somewhat bent figure that we have just depicted, M. de Fontanis displayed a narrow occiput, not very low and rising to a distinct eminence, adorned by a yellow forehead magisterially covered by a multi-layered wig, of a kind that had never yet been seen in Paris; two rather bandy legs supported, with some magnificence, this walking church-tower, from whose chest – not without some inconvenience for those nearby – there issued the exhalations of a yelping voice that poured forth, with a certain pomposity, long compliments, half-French and half-Provençal, at which he never failed to smile himself, his mouth gaping so wide that it was possible to see as far as the uvula that dangled over a blackish chasm, entirely toothless, excoriated in various places, and bearing quite a resemblance to the opening of a certain seat that, given the structure of our weak and feeble humanity, is as often the throne of kings as of shepherds.

Quite apart from his physical attractions, M. de Fontanis had pretensions to wit; after dreaming one night that he had risen, with Saint Paul, to the third heaven, he thought himself the finest astronomer in France;[6] he argued on legislation like Farinacius and Cujas,[7] and you often heard him saying, as did these great men, and as do his colleagues who are not great men, that the life of a citizen, his fortune, his honour, his family – everything, in short, that society regards as sacred, is nothing in comparison with the detection of a crime, and that it is a hundred times better to risk the lives of fifteen innocents than to make the unfortunate error of saving a single guilty person, since heaven is just, even if *parlements* are not, and there is only one drawback to punishing an innocent person, namely that it sends a soul to paradise, whereas saving a guilty person risks allowing crime to flourish on earth. Only one class of individuals had any rights over the armour-clad soul of M. de Fontanis, namely, prostitutes; not that he made much use of them in general: although of an ardent temperament, his faculties were overeager and left him wanting more, and his desires always extended much further than his powers. M. de Fontanis merely aspired to the glory of transmitting his illustrious name to posterity, but what obliged this celebrated magistrate to show indulgence towards the priestesses of Venus was his claim that there were few female citizens more useful to the State, and that thanks to their deceit, their imposture and their wagging tongues, a throng of secret crimes could be revealed, and M. de Fontanis had this one good quality: he was a sworn enemy of everything that philosophers call 'human weakness'.

This somewhat grotesque assemblage of an Ostrogothic body and a Justinian morality[8] left the town of Aix for the first time in April 1779 and, summoned by the Baron de Téroze, whom he had known for a long time (for various reasons of little importance to the reader), stayed in the Hôtel de Danemark, not far from the Baron's house.[9] As this was the time of the Saint-Germain fair,[10] everyone in the hotel thought that this extraordinary animal was here to be put on display. One of those officious people who are forever offering their services in these public establishments even offered to go and fetch Nicolet, who would be really delighted to prepare a place in the theatre for him, unless he preferred to make his debut at Audinot's.[11] The President said,* 'My maid warned me indeed, when I was a small boy, that you Parisians were a caustic and facetious people who would never do justice to my virtues; still, my wig-maker added that my scruffy old wig would impress them. Ah, the common people – how good they are! They joke when they are dying of starvation, and they sing when they are being crushed… Oh, I have always said as much: what these folk need is an Inquisition, as in Madrid, or a scaffold always standing ready, as in Aix.'

However, M. de Fontanis, after a brief session attending to his toilet, which did not fail to heighten his sexagenarian charms, and after several sprayings of rose water and lavender that were not, as Horace says, unduly ambitious adornments[12] – after all this, and perhaps a few other precautions that have not reached our attention, the President came to present himself at the home of his friend the old Baron; the double doors opened wide, he was announced, and the President entered. Unfortunately for him, the two sisters and the Count

---

* The reader is warned that the President's whole role should be pronounced with a Provençal accent, rolling the 'r's even though the spelling does not indicate this. [Sade's note. It is curious that he here seems to be giving instructions to the reader to 'perform' the story mentally, as if it were a play, and taking care that the reader hear the President's words in the right accent.]

d'Olincourt were all three having as much fun as real children in one corner of the salon when this unlikely figure made his appearance, and despite their best efforts, they could not contain their laughter, whereupon the grave countenance of the Provençal magistrate found itself most seriously discomposed; he had studied his entrance bow for a long time in front of a mirror, and he was giving quite a passable version of it when the cursed guffaw that escaped from our young friends almost made the President remain bent double for much longer than he had purposed. However, he rose; a stern glance from the Baron at his three children brought them back within the boundaries of respect, and the conversation began.

The Baron, who was intent on getting to the point as quickly as possible, and whose mind was already made up, did not allow this first interview to go by without informing Mlle de Téroze that this was the husband he had chosen for her, and that she was to give him her hand in marriage within a week at the latest; Mlle de Téroze did not utter a word, the President withdrew and the Baron repeated that he expected his wishes to be obeyed. It was a cruel situation: not only did this beautiful girl adore M. d'Elbène, not only was she in turn idolised by him, but, being as weak as she was impressionable, she had unfortunately already allowed her charming suitor to pluck that flower that, quite unlike roses (although the two are often compared), does not, as do roses, have the ability to blossom anew each spring. Now, whatever would M. de Fontanis have said – a President of the *Parlement* of Aix – if he had found that someone had already carried out his conjugal duty for him? A Provençal magistrate is allowed to have his comical defects – you expect them in such a class of people – but he does know untouched fruits when he sees them, and he is all too happy to be the first to harvest them at least once in his life – namely, in the woman he marries. This is what gave Mlle de Téroze pause, for, although lively and mischievous in character, she had all the delicacy of soul that behoves a woman in such cases, and she sensed full well that her husband would have little esteem for her if he became convinced that she had disrespected him even before she had got to know him, for nothing is as justified as our prejudices on this issue: not only is it necessary for an unfortunate girl to sacrifice all the sentiments of her heart to the husband that her parents give her, but she is even guilty if, before making the acquaintance of the tyrant who is to enslave her, she has so much as listened to nature and contrived to yield for a single moment to its voice. So Mlle de Téroze confided her sorrows and anxieties to her sister who, being much more playful than prudish and much more amiable than devout, started to laugh uproariously at the secret she had just been told and immediately shared it with her grave husband, who decided that since things were in such a state of ruin and disrepair, they must at all costs never be mentioned to the priests of Themis,[13] since those gentlemen never made light of matters of such importance, and his poor little sister would no sooner have arrived in the town where *the scaffold is always standing ready* than she would perhaps be forced to mount it, as a victim of the demands of chastity. Thereupon the Marquis came out with some apt quotations, especially after dinner (for he was sometimes capable of erudition), proving that the people of Provence were once an Egyptian colony, that the Egyptians very frequently sacrificed young girls, and that a President of the *Parlement* of Aix, being originally no more than a settler from Egypt, could without any miracle order his little sister's neck to be cut, even if it was the prettiest neck in the world.

'They're head-choppers, those magistrates from overseas; they'll slice through your neck just as easily as a crow pecks off walnuts,' continued d'Olincourt. 'And as for whether they are acting justly or not, they do not examine the matter too closely. Unbending severity, like Themis, wears a bandage round her eyes, placed there by stupidity, and in the town of Aix it is never removed by the good offices of philosophy.'[14]

So they agreed to hold a meeting: the Count, the Marquis, Madame d'Olincourt and her charming sister went to dine in a little house belonging to the Marquis in the Bois de Boulogne, and here, the stern Areopagus[15] decided, in an enigmatic style resembling the replies of the Cumaean Sibyll,[16] or the decrees of the *Parlement* of Aix (which by virtue of its Egyptian birthright has some right to resort to hieroglyphs), that it was necessary that the President both *wed* and *not wed*. Once this verdict had been reached and the actors told what to say, they returned to the Baron's; the young girl made no difficulties to her father, d'Olincourt and his wife looked forward with eager anticipation, so they claimed, to such a well-matched marriage, and they fooled the President to the top of his bent, taking care not to laugh again when he appeared; thus they so won over the minds of son-in-law and father-in-law that they persuaded them both to agree that the only place for the mysteries of Hymen to be celebrated was d'Olincourt's chateau near Melun, a splendid estate belonging to the Marquis. Everyone concurred; the Baron alone was, so he said, sorry not to be able to join in the pleasures of such a delightful celebration, but if he could, he would go and see them. At last the day arrived; the bride and groom were sacramentally united at Saint-Sulpice, very early in the morning, without the least pomp or circumstance, and the very same day they left for the chateau of d'Olincourt.

The Count d'Elbène had disguised himself, assuming the name and the dress of La Brie, the Marquise's manservant; he received the company when they arrived, and once supper was over, led the newly-weds to the nuptial chamber, whose decorations and machines had all been arranged by him; he was responsible for operating them.[17]

'In truth, my little darling,' said the amorous Provençal as soon as he saw himself all alone with his bride, 'your charms are those of Venus herself, strewth!* I do not know from whence you have acquired them, but one could travel the length and breadth of Provence without ever finding your equal.'

Then, he started fondling poor little Téroze through her skirts: she did not know whether to succumb to laughter or alarm. 'And this bit here and that bit there, God damn me;[18] and you can count me no judge of whores if these are not the very shapes of Eros beneath the gleaming petticoats of his mother.'

But at that moment La Brie came in bearing two deep golden goblets, presented one to the young bride and offered the other to the President.

'Drink, chaste newly-weds!' he said. 'And may you both find in this draught the presents of love and the gifts of Hymen.'

When the magistrate enquired what this drink was for, La Brie replied, 'Monsieur le Président, this is a Parisian custom that goes back to the baptism of Clovis: it is the custom among us that, before celebrating the mysteries upon which you will both soon be engaged, you might draw from this lenitive, purified by the blessing of the bishop, the strength necessary for the enterprise.'

---

* A Provençal oath. [Sade's note. Fontanis actually says *caspita!*]

'Ah, dammit, all too glad to,' replied the man of law, 'give it here, my friend, give it here… But bigod, if you intend to fan my flames, let your young mistress look out for herself, I am only too primed for action already, and if you bring me to the point where I lose my self-control, I do not know what will happen.'

The President swallowed the draught, his young bride followed his example, the manservant withdrew and the couple went to bed, but no sooner were they in it than the President was seized by such griping pains in the entrails, and such an urgent need to relieve his weak and feeble nature on the side opposite the one that should have been dis-charging its duties, that without reflecting on where he was, and without the least respect for the woman sharing his bed, he flooded the bed and its environs with such a considerable deluge of bile that Mlle de Téroze, panic-stricken, only just had time to jump out and call for help. People rushed up, M. and Mme d'Olincourt, who had deliberately stayed awake, dashed in, and the President, deeply embarrassed, wrapped himself in the sheets so as not to make an exhibition of him-self, paying no heed to the fact that the more he concealed his person, the more soiled he became, and he eventually became such an object of horror and disgust that his young bride and everyone present withdrew, expressing their deepest sympathy for his state and assuring him that they would that very same minute inform the Baron so that he could immediately send to the chateau one of the best doctors in the capital.

'Oh good heavens!' exclaimed the poor President in con-sternation, as soon as he was alone, 'what an unexpected turn of events! I thought it was only in our law courts, and on fleurs-de-lis, that we could overflow like this – but on one's wedding night, in the wench's bed, now that is something I really cannot understand!'

A lieutenant from d'Olincourt's regiment, named Delgatz, who had followed two or three courses at veterinary school so he could attend to the needs of the regiment's horses, did not fail to arrive the next day, having assumed the name and title of one of the most celebrated sons of Aesculapius[19]. Monsieur de Fontanis had been advised to appear in informal costume, and Mme la Présidente de Fontanis – to whom, however, we should not yet grant that name[20] – did not conceal from her husband how attractive she found him in this dress: he was wearing a dressing gown of yellow calamanco with red stripes down to the waist, adorned with facings and lapels, and beneath this a little waistcoat of coarse brown muslin, with sailor's breeches of the same colour, and a red woollen bonnet; all of this, set off by the alluring pallor from his accident the night before, inspired Mlle de Téroze with such a redoubled access of love that she refused to leave him for so much as a quarter of an hour.

'Crikey!' the President kept saying,[21] 'how she loves me! In truth, here is the woman that heaven had destined for my happiness; I rather misbehaved last night, but we do not get diarrhoea every day.'[22]

Meanwhile the doctor arrived. He felt his patient's pulse, and was surprised to find how weak it was; he demonstrated by the aphorisms of Hippocrates and the commentaries of Galen that unless he restored his strength that evening, supping on half a dozen bottles of Spanish wine or Madeira, it would be impossible for him to succeed in the proposed deflowering; as for the indigestion of the night before, he assured him it was nothing.

'It comes, Monsieur,' he said, 'from the fact that the bile had not been filtered through the ducts of the liver.'

'But this accident was not dangerous,' said the Marquis.

'Pardon me, Monsieur,' replied the votary of the Temple of Epidauros[23] gravely, 'in medicine there is no such thing as a small cause that may not turn into something serious unless the deep mysteries of our art do not straightaway suspend its effects. From this trifling accident, a considerable deterioration in Monsieur's organisation might ensue; this unfiltered bile, carried by the arch of the aorta into the sub-clavicle artery, transported thence into the delicate membranes of the brain via the carotids, might have affected the circulation of the animal spirits and suspended their natural activity, thereby producing madness.'

'Oh heavens,' replied Mlle de Téroze bursting into tears, 'my husband, mad! Oh sister, my husband – mad!'

'Calm yourself, Madame, it is nothing, thanks to my swift intervention, and I will now promise you I can cure the patient.'

On these words, joy was seen to spread anew in every heart, and the Marquis d'Olincourt tenderly embraced his brother-in-law, and demonstrated to him in a warm and provincial manner how concerned he was for his welfare. Then all minds turned to pleasure. That day, the Marquis received his vassals and his neighbours, and the President wanted to dress up for the occasion; but he was dissuaded from doing so, and they enjoyed showing him off in the clothes he was wearing to all the society in the neighbourhood.

'Ah, how charming he is like that!' the wicked Marquise would say at every opportunity. 'Indeed, M. d'Olincourt, if I had known before I made your acquaintance that the sovereign magistracy of Aix included such agreeable people as my brother-in-law, I must confess that I would have married none but a member of that respectable assembly.'

And the President thanked her repeatedly, bowing and smiling unpleasantly, sometimes simpering before the mirrors and quietly saying to himself, '*There is no doubt about it: I am not at all bad-looking.*' Finally, supper time arrived; they had invited the cursed doctor to stay; he himself drank like a Switzer, and had no difficulty in persuading his patient to follow his example; care had been taken to place a selection of heady wines within reach, which quickly muddled their brains and soon brought the President to the state in which they wanted to see him. They rose from table, and the lieutenant, who had played his role exceedingly well, made his way to bed, and disappeared the following day; as for our hero, his young wife took him in hand and led him to the nuptial bed; the whole society escorted him in triumph, and the Marquise, as charming as ever (even more, indeed, when she had been emptying champagne into herself), assured him that he had indulged a little too much and that she was afraid that, overheated by the fumes of Bacchus, he would not be bound by the chains of Love that night.

'That is nothing, Madame la Marquise,' replied the President. 'Those gods of seduction merely become even more redoubtable when they join forces; as far as reason is concerned, whether it be lost in wine or in the flames of love, since we can do without it, what difference does it make to which of those two divinities we have sacrificed? We magistrates find that reason is the easiest thing in the world to dispense with; banished from our law courts as it is from our heads, we delight in trampling it underfoot, and that is what makes our judicial sentences such masterpieces, since (although commonsense never presides in them) those sentences are carried out with as much firmness as if people knew what they actually meant. As you see me, Madame la

Marquise,' continued the President, tottering slightly, and picking up his red bonnet, which a momentary loss of balance had just separated from his hairless skull… 'Yes, truly, as you see me, I have one of the best brains in my troop; I it was, last year, who persuaded my witty colleagues to exile from the province for ten years, thereby ruining him forever, a gentleman who had always served his king – and all because he entertained himself with whores: there was some resistance, but I pronounced my opinion, and the troop yielded at the sound of my voice… Gadzooks, look you, I like decent behaviour, I like temperance and sobriety, and everything that shocks those two virtues revolts me, and my wrath breaks forth; one must be severe, severity is the daughter of justice… and justice is the mother of… Pardon me, Madame, there are moments when my memory sometimes leaves me in the lurch…'

'Yes, yes, quite so,' replied the skittish Marquise as she left, taking everyone with her, 'just make sure that not everything plays you false like your memory this evening, since it is time to bring things to a conclusion, and my little sister who adores you would not put up forever with such abstinence.'

'You have nothing to fear, Madame, nothing to fear,' replied the President, trying to see the Marquise out, though his gait was somewhat circumflex, 'do not worry, I beg you; tomorrow I will present her to you as the real Madame de Fontanis, just as surely as I am a man of honour. Is that not so, my girl,' continued the man of the robe as he returned to his companion, 'do you not grant that this night will consummate our labours?… You see how greatly it is desired, there is not a single member of your family who does not feel honoured to be allied to me: nothing is so flattering as to have a magistrate in the household.'

17

'Who could doubt it, Monsieur?' replied the young girl. 'I can assure you that, as far as I am concerned, I have never felt so proud as since I have heard myself being called Madame la Présidente.'

'I can believe it all too well; come now, get undressed, light of my life, I feel a little heavy-headed, and I would like, if possible, to complete our operation before sleep comes to carry me off completely.'

But as Mlle de Téroze, as is customary among newly-wed brides, just could not finish dressing for bed, never finding what she needed, scolding her women and taking forever over the task, the President could not hold out, decided to go to bed, and contented himself with shouting for a quarter of an hour, 'Come on now, dammit! I just cannot imagine what you are up to, it will soon be too late.'

However, nothing happened, and since, given the state of intoxication of our modern Lycurgus,[24] it was really rather difficult to find himself with his head on a pillow without falling asleep, he yielded to this most pressing of needs, and was already snoring as if he had been passing sentence on some whore from Marseilles – and Mlle de Téroze had not even changed into her nightdress.

'He is just as he should be,' said the Count d'Elbène, creeping into the bedroom. 'Come, my darling, come and bestow upon me the moments of happiness which that gross beast would like to steal from us.'

With these words, he led away the lovely subject of his idolatry; the lights in the nuptial apartment were extinguished, its polished floor was immediately covered with mattresses, and at a given signal, the portion of the bed occupied by our magistrate was separated from the rest and, by the means of a few pulleys, raised twenty feet into the air: the soporific state in which our legislator lay did not allow him to notice a thing. Meanwhile, at around three in the morning, awoken by the discomfort of a rather full bladder, and remembering that he had seen next to the bed a table where stood the vessel necessary for him to relieve himself in, he fumbled around; surprised at first to find nothing but emptiness on every side, he bent forward; but the bed, supported only by ropes, followed the movements of the man who was leaning over in it, and finally gave way entirely, completely tipping over and vomiting, right into the middle of the bedroom, the load weighing it down: the President fell onto the mattresses placed in preparation, and his surprise was so great that he started to howl like a calf being led to the slaughterhouse.

'Ah, what the devil is this?' he said to himself. 'Madame, Madame, you are here, are you not? Well, can you explain this fall? Last night I went to bed four feet above the ground, and now, when I need my chamber pot, I fall from a height of over twenty feet.'

But nobody replied to these tender plaints, and the President who, if truth be told, did not find his new bed all that uncomfortable, abandoned his investigation and ended his night there, as if he had been lying in his shabby bed in Provence. After his fall, they had made sure to lower the bed gently down again so that, fitting back into the part from which it had been separated, it seemed to form just one single couch, and at nine in the morning, Mlle de Téroze crept back into the room; no sooner was she there than she opened all the windows and rang for her women.

'To tell you the truth, Monsieur,' she said to the President, 'you are not very agreeable company, you have to admit, and I am certainly going to complain to my family about the way you are treating me.'

'What is all this?' said the President, sobering up, rubbing his eyes and quite unable to understand how it was that he happened to be lying on the floor.

'What? I will tell you what this is!' said his young bride, doing her best to feign annoyance. 'Whenever, impelled by the feelings that are to bind me to you, I approached your person last night to receive the assurances of the same sentiments on your part, you thrust me roughly away and flung me onto the ground…'

'Ah, good heavens,' said the President, 'look, my girl, I am starting to understand how it all might have happened… a thousand apologies… Last night, I had an urgent need and was looking everywhere for some means to satisfy it, and as I rolled this way and that and fell out of bed, I must have pushed you out too; I am all the more excusable in that I was certainly dreaming, since I imagined I had fallen from a height of more than twenty feet. Come now, it is nothing, it is nothing, my angel, we must postpone our enjoyments until tonight, and I assure you that I will do my duty; I will drink nothing but water; but just give me a kiss, my sweetheart, let us make peace before we appear in front of the public, or else I will think you are harbouring a grudge against me, and I would not want that for a whole kingdom.'

Mademoiselle de Téroze was perfectly prepared to offer one of her rosy cheeks, still glowing from the fires of love, to the foul kisses of that old faun; the company entered and the newly-weds took care to conceal the unfortunate nocturnal catastrophe.

The whole day passed by in enjoyment, and in particular in a long walk that, taking M. de Fontanis far from the chateau, gave La Brie time to prepare new scenes. The President was now resolved to consummate his wedding, and was so careful during his meals that it proved impossible to make use of such methods to waylay his reason, but fortunately they had more than one cog in the wheel to turn, and the noteworthy Fontanis had too many sworn enemies for him to be able to evade their trap. Everyone went to bed.

'Ah, this night, my angel,' said the President to his young bride, 'I flatter myself that you will not escape.'

But for all his bravado, it was of course necessary that the weapons with which he was menacing her should be in good shape, and since he wished to present himself for the assault in the regular way, the poor Provençal lay, in his corner of the bed, making the most incredible efforts... He stretched and stiffened, all his sinews were in a state of contraction... and this made him press himself against his bed with two or three times as much strength as if he had been lying there at rest, so that his efforts finally made the booby-trapped beams in the ceiling below give way, and the unfortunate magistrate was toppled into a pigsty that was right under his bedroom. This gave rise to a long discussion among those gathered at the d'Olincourt chateau as to who must have been the most surprised – the President, on thus finding himself among animals that were so common in his homeland, or those same animals on finding one of the most famous magistrates of the *Parlement* of Aix in their company. Several people claimed that the satisfaction must have been equal on both sides: in fact, the President must certainly have been in seventh heaven on finding himself, so to speak, among his own kind, breathing for a moment the tangy odour of his own native soil, and for their part the impure animals forbidden by the good Moses[25] must have given thanks to heaven on finding, at last, a legislator at their head – and a legislator of the *Parlement* of Aix, who, accustomed from his youth to sit in judgment on cases relating to the favourite element of these fine beasts, might one day so settle matters as to forestall the need for any further discussions on this element that is so analogous to the organisms of both parties.

Be that as it may, since it took a while for the parties to become acquainted, and as civilisation, the mother of politeness, is barely any more advanced among the members of the *Parlement* of Aix than it is among the animals despised by the Israelite, there was, to begin with, a kind of clash of arms in which the President won no laurels: he was beaten, buffeted, harassed by aggressive snouts; he remonstrated, but they did not listen; he promised to record the deed, but there was no reply; he spoke of a writ, but this too failed to impress them; he threatened them with exile, and they trampled him underfoot; and the wretched Fontanis, covered in blood, was already wording a sentence involving nothing less than the stake, when people finally rushed in to help him.

It was La Brie and the colonel who, armed with torches, had come to try and extricate the magistrate from the mire in which he lay engulfed, but they first needed to decide which end to pick him up by, and as he was completely covered with the stuff from head to feet, it was neither very easy nor very fragrant to grab hold of him. La Brie went to get a fork, a groom was hastily summoned to bring another, and in this way they managed to pull him, as best they could, clear of the muck of the vile cesspit in which his fall had buried him… But where were they to take him now? That was the problem, and it was not an easy one to solve. They needed to purge the writ, the guilty party must be cleared and cleansed, and the colonel proposed letters of rescission, but the groom, who understood none of all these grand words, said that he should simply be placed for a couple of hours in the water trough, and after that, once he had had an adequate soak, a few handfuls of straw would turn him into a handsome figure of a man once more. But the Marquis insisted that the coldness of the water might have a deleterious affect on his brother's health,[26] whereupon La Brie assured them that the kitchen boy's scullery was still equipped with hot water, so there they took the President, and entrusted him to the care of that pupil of Comus,[27] who in less than no time made him as clean as a china bowl.

'I do not suggest you go back to your wife,' said d'Olincourt as soon as he saw the man of the robe all soaped and scrubbed, 'I know how delicate your feelings are; so La Brie will take you to a small bachelor room where you will be able to spend the rest of the night in peace and quiet.'

'Very well, my dear Marquis,' said the President, 'I agree to your proposal… But you have to admit, someone must have put a spell on me for such a series of adventures to befall me like this on every night since I first arrived in this damned chateau.'

'There is a natural cause behind it all,' said the Marquis; 'the doctor will come back to see us tomorrow; my advice is that you consult him.'

'Gladly,' replied the President, and went to his little bedroom with La Brie. When he got there, he said to him, as he climbed into bed, 'The fact is, my friend, that I had never been so close to my goal.'

'Alas, Monsieur,' replied the cunning lad as he withdrew, 'it is heaven that must have decreed these things; let me tell you that you have my deepest sympathy.'

Delgatz had felt the President's pulse and assured him that the breaking of the wooden beams was simply the result of an excess of engorgement in the lymph vessels, which, doubling the mass of the humours, had doubled his animal volume;

in consequence, he needed to follow an austere diet, which would purify the bitterness of the humours, inevitably diminish his physical weight and contribute to the success of his plans, and furthermore…

'But Monsieur,' interrupted Fontanis, 'I have dislocated my hip, and put out my left arm in that dreadful fall…'

'I can well believe it,' replied the doctor, 'but those side effects are not at all the ones that cause me the most alarm; I always go back to the causes, you need to get your blood working, Monsieur; by reducing the bitterness of the lymph, we free up the vessels, and as the circulation in the vessels becomes easier, we inevitably reduce the physical mass, and as a result, ceilings will no longer collapse under your weight, and you will be able from now on to go to bed and indulge in all the exercises you wish without running any further risks.'

'And what about my arm, Monsieur, and my hip?'

'Let us purge you, Monsieur, let us purge you, and then let us try a couple of local bloodlettings and everything will gradually get better.'

That very same day, the diet began; Delgatz, who did not leave his patient all week, put him on thin chicken broth, and purged him three times in succession, forbidding him even to think of his wife. Despite his being a total ignoramus, Lieutenant Delgatz's treatment was a marvellous success; he assured everyone there that previously, while working at the veterinary school, he had prescribed exactly the same for a donkey who had fallen down a very deep hole, and after a month the animal was fully recovered and cheerfully carrying along his sacks of plaster, as had been his wont. And indeed, the President, who continued to suffer from an excess of bile, was nonetheless soon fresh and ruddy-cheeked again; his bruises faded, and they devoted all their efforts to making him better, so as to give him the strength he would require in order to endure the coming ordeal.

On the twelfth day of the treatment, Delgatz took his patient by the hand and presented him to Mlle de Téroze, saying, 'Here he is, Madame, here he is, that man so refractory to the laws of Hippocrates, I am handing him over to you, safe and sound, and if he indulges without let or hindrance in the strength I have restored in him, we will have the pleasure of seeing you, within six months' – continued Delgatz, gently placing his hand on Mlle de Téroze's belly… 'yes, Madame, we will all have the satisfaction of seeing this lovely womb starting to swell, thanks to the good offices of Hymen.'

'May God grant your prayer, Doctor,' replied the mischievous girl, 'you must admit that it is really rather hard for a woman to have been married for a fortnight and yet still be a virgin.'

'It is beyond belief,' said the President. 'One does not get indigestion every night, nor is it every night that the need to urinate tips a husband out of his bed, and when one thinks one is falling into the arms of a pretty woman, one does not usually straightaway fall headlong into a pigsty.'

'We shall see about that,' said the young Téroze, heaving a deep sigh, 'we shall see, Monsieur, but the fact is, if you loved me as much as I love you, all those misfortunes would not befall you.'

Supper was a very merry affair, and the Marquise was agreeable if rather impish, wagering against her husband that her brother-in-law would carry out his task successfully, and everyone retired. They hastily dressed for bed, and Mlle de Téroze modestly begged her husband not to allow any light in the room; the latter, too cowed to refuse her anything, granted her all that she desired, and they went to bed. This time, there were no obstacles: the intrepid President triumphed, and plucked – or so he thought – that precious flower to which so much value is foolishly attached; five times in succession he was crowned by love, and finally, as day broke, the windows were opened, and the rays of the daystar that they allowed to come flooding into the bedroom finally offered to the victor's eyes the spectacle of the victim he had just immolated… Good heavens! What did he think when he discovered an old Negro woman lying in his wife's place, and saw a face as black as it was hideous replacing the delicate features he imagined he had just possessed!

He recoiled, crying out that someone had put a spell on him; whereupon his wife arrived, and, discovering him in bed with that divinity of Tenaros,[28] asked him sharply what wrong she could have done him to make him betray her so cruelly.

'But, Madame, was it not with you that yesterday…'

'I, Monsieur? *I*, shamed and humiliated as I am, have no need to reproach myself in the least for having failed to be your submissive servant; you saw this woman next to me, you thrust me brutally away to lay your hands on her, you forced her to occupy my place in the bed that was meant for me, and I retired in perplexity, with only my tears for relief.'

'But tell me, my angel, are you quite sure of all the facts you are alleging here?'

'Ah, the monster! Now he wants to add insult to injury! And sarcasm is my reward, when I had hoped to find consolation… Come hither, my sister; let my whole family come and see the unworthy being to whom I have been sacrificed… There she is… there she is, that odious rival!' exclaimed the young wife whose rights had been thwarted; a flood of tears was pouring from her eyes. 'He dares to lie in her arms, right in front of my eyes! Ah, my friends,' continued

Mlle de Téroze in despair, gathering the whole household around her, 'help me, lend me weapons against this traitor. Was *this* what I was supposed to expect, when I adored him as I did?'

Nothing could have been more comical than Fontanis's face as he listened in amazement to these words. From time to time he gazed in bewilderment at his Negro woman; then he turned his gaze to his young wife, and stared at her with a sort of idiotic absorption, which could really have started to have a worrying effect on the disposition of his brain. By a singular quirk of fate, ever since the President had been at the chateau of d'Olincourt, La Brie (that rival in disguise whom he should most have feared) had of all people there become the one whom he trusted the most. He called him over.

'My friend,' he said, 'you have always struck me as a sensible lad; would you do me the pleasure of telling me if you really have noticed any worsening in the condition of my brain?'

'My word, Monsieur le Président,' replied La Brie, looking sad and perplexed, 'I would never had dared tell you so, but since you do me the honour of asking me for my opinion, I will not conceal from you that ever since you fell into the pigs' trough, your ideas have never come out quite right from the membranes of your cerebellum; do not let that worry you, Monsieur, the doctor who has already treated you is one of the greatest men we have ever had in this area… Look, we once had the judge from the estates of Monsieur le Marquis in this part of the world; he had gone so mad that there was not a single young libertine in the area who could enjoy himself with a woman without that rascal immediately charging him with a crime, issuing a writ and sentencing him to exile and coming out with all the platitudes those rascals are always spouting; well, Monsieur, our doctor, that universal man who has already had the honour of treating you with eighteen bloodlettings and thirty-two medicines, has made his brain as healthy as if he had never sat as a judge in his whole life. But look,' continued La Brie, turning round on hearing a noise, '"speak of the devil and he appears", as the saying goes… Here's the fellow in person!'

'Ah, good day, my dear Doctor,' said the Marquise on seeing Delgatz arrive. 'To tell you the truth, I think we have never had so much need of your ministerings; our dear friend the President suffered yesterday evening from a slight brain disturbance that, in spite of all present, made him take this Negro woman instead of his wife.'

'In spite of all present?' said the President. 'What – you mean people really tried to prevent it?'

'I myself was the first to do so, and with all my strength,' replied La Brie, 'but Monsieur was going at it so vigorously that I preferred to let him get on with it rather than expose myself to being maltreated by Monsieur.'

Whereupon, the President rubbed his head. He was starting to feel utterly at a loss, when the doctor went over to him and felt his pulse.

'This is more serious than the last accident,' said Delgatz, lowering his eyes. 'It is an unexpected residue from our last illness – a smothered fire that escapes the intelligent gaze of the specialist and breaks out just when one least expects it. There is a definite obstruction in the diaphragm and a prodigious erethism[29] in the whole organism.'

'A heretism?' cried the President in a rage. 'Whatever is that rascal talking about with his "heretism"? Just you listen to me, you bounder: I have never been a heretic, and it is easy to see, you old fool, that you know next to nothing about the history of France, otherwise you would be aware that if anyone burns heretics, *we* do! Take a tour of our region, you misbegotten foundling from Salerno,[30] go, my friend, and see Mérondil and Cabrières still smouldering from the fires we lit there;[31] take a walk through the rivers of blood that the respectable members of our law courts shed in such torrents through the province; you can still hear the groans of the wretches whom we immolated to our fury, the sobs of the women we tore from the bosoms of their husbands, the screams of the children we slaughtered in their mothers' wombs. Finally, take a close look at all of the holy horrors that we committed, and you will see whether, after the prudent measures we took, it behoves an imbecile like you to treat us as heretics!'

The President, still in bed with the Negro woman, had in the heat of his narration given her such a rough punch on the nose that the unhappy woman fled, howling like a bitch whose puppies are being taken from her.

'Look now, look now – a fit of madness, my friend?' said d'Olincourt, going over to the patient. 'Is this any way to behave, President? As you can see, your health is taking a turn for the worse and it is essential for you to look after yourself.'

'That is more like it! When people speak to me like that, I will listen, but to hear myself being treated as a heretic by that charlatan of Saint-Côme,[32] well, you will admit that is something I simply cannot tolerate.'

'He had no intention of doing so, my dear brother,' said the Marquise gently; '"erethism" is the synonym for "inflammation"; it was never another word for "heresy"'.

'Ah, my apologies, Madame la Marquise, my apologies, I am sometimes a little hard of hearing. Come, let this grave disciple of Averroes[33] step forward and speak, I will listen… No, I will do more, I will do whatever he tells me to do.'

29

Delgatz, whom the President's eruption of fury had driven away, lest he meet with the same treatment as the Negro woman, came back over to the edge of the bed.

'I will say it again, Monsieur,' said the new Galen as he felt his patient's pulse again, 'great erethism in the organism.'

'He-re-...?'

'*Erethism*, Monsieur,' the doctor said quickly, ducking to avoid a punch. 'I therefore conclude that you need a rapid phlebotomy of the jugular, followed by a few repeated ice-cold baths.'

'I do not altogether agree with the bloodletting,' said d'Olincourt. 'Monsieur le Président is no longer of an age to tolerate that sort of assault without there being a very good reason; in any case, I do not share the bloodthirsty mania of the children of Themis and Aesculapius; my system is that there are just as few illnesses for which blood should be let as there are crimes for which it should be shed. President, you will agree with me (I hope) when it is a matter of sparing yours – I might, perhaps, not be quite so certain of your opinion if you had a less personal interest in the matter.'

'Monsieur,' replied the President, 'I agree with the first half of what you said, but allow me to disagree strongly with the second: it is with blood that crime is wiped out, with blood alone that crime is atoned for and deterred. Compare, Monsieur, all the evils that crime can produce on earth with the much lesser evil of a dozen or so malefactors executed per year in order to deter them.'

'Your paradox does not have commonsense on its side, my friend,' said d'Olincourt. 'It is dictated by severity and stupidity; it is a vice that belongs to your profession and your native region, and you ought to abjure it once and for all. Quite apart from the fact that your idiotic severities have never once prevented a crime, it is absurd to say that one misdeed can make up for another and that the death of a second man can in any way redress that of a first. You and your sort should blush at these ways of thinking, which do not prove your integrity so much as they do your overmastering taste for despotism; people are right to call you the tormentors of the human race: your combined efforts alone destroy more men than all natural disasters put together.'

'Messieurs,' said the Marquise, 'it strikes me that this is neither the time nor the place for a discussion of this sort; instead of calming my young brother, Monsieur,' she continued, turning to her husband, 'you are merely inflaming his blood even more, and you risk making his illness incurable.'

'Madame la Marquise is right,' said the doctor. 'Allow me, Monsieur, to order La Brie to go and put forty pounds of ice in the bathtub that will then be filled with water from the well, and during the time it takes to prepare, I will give my patient an enema.'

Everyone immediately withdrew; the President got up, and quibbled for a while longer over the ice-cold bath that, he said, would make him good for nothing for at least six weeks, but there was no way of escaping; down he went, they immersed him in it, and forced him to stay in for ten to twelve minutes, in front of the eyes of all present, gathered from the whole neighbourhood to enjoy the scene, and once the patient had been dried down, he dressed and reappeared in the assembly as if nothing at all had happened.

Straight after dinner, the Marquise suggested they go for a walk.

'Fresh air must be good for the President, do you not think, Doctor?' she asked Delgatz.

'Assuredly,' replied the latter. 'Madame must be aware that there are no asylums without a courtyard in which the lunatics can take the air.'

'I flatter myself,' said the President, 'that you do not think I am altogether a lost cause.'

'Not in the least, Monsieur,' replied Delgatz, 'it is but a slight mental upset; so long as it is nipped in the bud, it should not have any ill effects, but Monsieur le Président must remain cool and calm.'

'What is that, Monsieur – do you think that this evening I will not be able to make a fresh attempt?'

'This evening, Monsieur? I shudder at the very idea; if I treated you with as much severity as you treat others, I would forbid you any commerce with women for three or four months.'

'Three or four months? Good heavens!…' And, turning to his wife, the President said, 'Three or four months, my darling; would you be able to hold out that long, my angel?'

'Oh, Monsieur Delgatz will soften his rigour, I hope,' replied the young Téroze with feigned naivety. 'He will at least take pity on me, even if he does not take pity on you…'

And they set off on their walk. There was a ferry they needed to take to cross over to the home of a gentleman who lived nearby, who was in on the plot and was expecting the company for a light repast; once they were in the boat, our young friends started to frolic around, and Fontanis, to please his wife, did not fail to follow suit.

'President,' said the Marquis, 'I bet you cannot hang from the boat's rope like me for several minutes at a stretch.'

'Nothing could be easier,' said the President, finishing his pinch of snuff and rising on tiptoe to get better hold of the rope.

'Oh excellent! Much better than you, my brother!' said young Téroze on seeing her husband hanging there.

But as the President hung there, showing off his gracefulness and skill, the boatmen, who had been given the signal, started rowing twice as fast, and the vessel sped swiftly away, leaving the unfortunate man suspended between the sky and the water...[34] He shouted and cried for help; they were only halfway across; there were still forty or fifty yards to go before reaching shore.

'Do the best you can!' they shouted back to him. 'Pull yourself to the shore – as you can see, the wind is carrying us away; it is impossible for us to get back to you!'

And the President thrashed and floundered and struggled, doing everything he could to catch up with the boat that was still speeding away as the rowers pulled hard; what a sight for sore eyes it was – to see one of the gravest magistrates of the *Parlement* of Aix hanging there in his big wig and his black robes.

'President!' the Marquis called to him roaring with laughter. 'This really is nothing more than a boon of Providence: an eye for an eye, my friend, that is the favourite law of your courts, so how can you complain at being thus hanged? Have you not frequently sentenced to the same punishment many others who had not deserved it any more than you?'

But the President could no longer hear him: dreadfully tired from the violent exertions imposed on him, his hands lost their grip, and he fell with a great splash into the water; at the same moment, two divers who had been kept ready for the occasion hastened to his aid, and he was hauled back on board, soaked to the skin, and cursing like a waggoner. Initially he tried to complain at this joke that he found quite out of place – but they swore to him that they had not been joking at all, a gust of wind had driven the boat away; they warmed him up in the boatman's hut, changed his clothes, and fussed round him; his young wife did everything she could to make him forget all about his little accident, and Fontanis, being in love, and weak, was soon laughing away with the rest of them at the spectacle he had just made of himself.

They finally arrived at the home of the gentleman they were visiting, and they were given a delightful reception, and the most copious repast was served; they contrived to get the President to swallow down a *crème aux pistaches*, and no sooner was it in his entrails than he was obliged to enquire there and then for the whereabouts of the privy; they showed him into one that was very dark; it was a matter of dreadful urgency, and he sat down and relieved himself as fast as he could, but once the operation was over, the President could no longer get up.

'What is all this?' he exclaimed, wriggling his backside…

But however hard he tried, unless he left his posterior behind, he would never pull himself away. In the mean time, his absence had caused quite a sensation, and everyone enquired where he could be; his cries, becoming audible, finally attracted the attention of the whole company, who gathered outside the fateful privy.

'What the devil has kept you here for so long, my friend?' d'Olincourt asked him. 'Are you suffering from an attack of colic?'

'Damn it all!' said the poor devil, making redoubled efforts to get up. 'Can you not see that I am stuck…?'

But in order to present an even more comical sight to the gathering, and to increase the efforts made by the President to get up from that cursed seat, they slipped under his buttocks a little spirit lamp that singed his hair and, burning him really quite severely at times, had him making the extraordinary leaps and jumps and pulling the most horrible faces. The more loudly they laughed, the angrier the President became; he hurled curses at the women and threatened the men, and the more enraged he grew, the funnier his sweaty, gleaming face looked. In his exertions, his wig had come away from his skull, and his bare occiput wrinkled even more comically in time with the contortions of his facial muscles. Finally the gentleman rushed in, apologising profusely to the President for not having warned him that this privy was in no fit state to receive him; he and his servants unstuck the unfortunate sufferer as well as they could, though not without his losing a circular strip of skin that, for all their efforts, remained attached to the toilet seat that the painters had soaked in strong glue so it would take the colouring they intended to paint it with.

'Really,' said Fontanis, reappearing as bold as brass, 'you are fortunate to have me here, and I am adding considerably to your gaiety.'

'That is unfair, my friend,' replied d'Olincourt. 'Why must you always blame us for the mishaps that Fortune sends to you? I thought one needed only have the halter of Themis for equity to become a natural virtue, but I can see that I was mistaken.'

'That is because you do not have a clear idea of what is called equity,' said the President. 'At the bar we acknowledge several sorts of equity; there is what is called relative equity, and personal equity…'

'Not so fast,' said the Marquis, 'I have never seen the virtue that is analysed so much being practised to anything like the same degree. What I call equity, my friend, is quite simply the law of nature; anyone who follows that law is just, and one becomes unjust only if one strays from it. Tell me, President, if you had indulged in some whimsical fancy in the privacy of your own home, would you find it very equitable if a band of clumsy idiots came bearing their torches into your household, poking and prying with their inquisitorial, treacherous questions, and bribing people to denounce some minor misdeeds quite pardonable at the age of thirty, taking advantage of these atrocious measures to destroy you, banish you, cast a slur on your good name, dishonour you and pillage your estate? Tell me, my friend, what do you think – would you find those scoundrels very equitable? If it is true that you accept the existence of a Supreme Being, would you adore that model of justice if he deployed it in this way against men, and would you not shudder at the thought of being subject to his law?'

'And what are you driving at, may I ask? Do you criticise us for seeking out crime?... But it is our duty!'

'That is not true. Your duty consists merely in punishing crime when it shows its face. Leave it to the stupid and ferocious maxims of the Inquisition to indulge in the mean and barbarous activity of actively seeking it out, like treacherous spies or vile informers. What citizen will ever be safe if, being surrounded by servants whom you have suborned, his honour or his life are at every moment in the hands of people who, merely because they are chafed by the chains they bear, imagine they will be able to throw them off or lighten their burden by betraying to you the man who has imposed those chains upon them? You will have increased the number of scoundrels in the State, you will end up with treacherous women, slanderous menservants and ungrateful children, you will have doubled the number of vices – and you will not have produced a single virtue.'

'It is not a matter of producing virtues, it is merely a question of destroying crime.'

'But your measures increase it.'

'Well spoken; but such is the law, and we must follow it: *we* are not members of the legislative, my dear Marquis, but of the *executive.*'

'No, President, say rather,' replied d'Olincourt, who was starting to become heated, 'that you are *executors*, indeed *unworthy executioners* who, being naturally the enemies of the State, take delight in nothing but obstructing its prosperity, hindering its happiness, undermining its glory and, for no reason at all, shedding the precious blood of its subjects.'

In spite of the two ice-cold baths that Fontanis had taken that day, bile is such a difficult thing to destroy in a man of law that the poor President was quivering with rage at hearing someone denigrate a profession he believed to be so very respectable: he could not imagine that what is called 'the magistracy' could be so viciously treated, and perhaps he would have riposted as roundly as a sailor from Marseilles, but the ladies came over and proposed that they all return home. The Marquise asked the President if he again needed to pay a visit to the privy.

'No, no, Madame,' replied the Marquis, 'this respectable magistrate does not always have colic; he must be forgiven if he took the attack rather seriously: a stirring of the entrails is considered a significant illness in Marseilles or Aix, and ever since we saw a band of rogues – colleagues of our big bold friend here – deciding that a few whores who had the colic must have been *poisoned*, it is not to be wondered at that colic is a serious matter for a magistrate from Provence.'[35]

Fontanis, who of all the judges had been the severest in the case that had covered the magistrates of Provence in everlasting shame, was in an almost indescribable state, stammering, stamping his feet, foaming at the mouth: he resembled mastiffs in a bullfight when they are unable to get at their adversary to bite him, and d'Olincourt seized his opportunity.

'Look at him, just look at him, Mesdames, and tell me, I beg you, whether you would envy the situation of an unfortunate gentleman who, confident in his innocence and good faith, saw fifteen hound dogs like this one yapping round his breeches.'

The President was about to fly into a real rage, but the Marquis, who did not want any scandal yet, had prudently taken his seat in his carriage, and left Mlle de Téroze to apply balm to the wounds he had just inflicted. She found it very hard to succeed in doing so, but finally managed; the ferry made the return crossing without the President having any desire to dance on the rope, and they arrived in peace and quiet at the chateau. They had supper, and the doctor took care to remind Fontanis of the necessity of remaining abstinent.

'My word, the reminder is quite superfluous,' said the President. 'How do you expect a man who has spent the night with a Negro woman, who was treated as a heretic in the morning and given an ice-cold bath for his lunch, who shortly afterwards fell into the river, who, finding himself stuck at stool like a Pierrot caught in glue, had his backside burnt to a cinder while he was passing his motions, and to whose face people have been impudent enough to say that judges who sought out crime were nothing but miserable rascals and that whores who had the colic had not actually been poisoned – how do you expect, I ask you, a man in such a position to have the slightest intention of deflowering a virgin?'

'I am very pleased to see you being so sensible,' said Delgatz, accompanying Fontanis into the little bachelor room that he occupied when he had no designs on his wife. 'I exhort you to carry on like this, and you will soon feel all the benefits that will result.'

The next day, the ice-cold baths started again: throughout the period during which they were applied, the President did not need to be reminded of the necessity for his abstinence, and the delightful Téroze was at least able to enjoy, during this time, all the pleasures of love in the arms of her charming d'Elbène. Finally, a fortnight later, Fontanis, feeling fully refreshed, started once more to play the gallant to his wife.

'Oh really, Monsieur,' said the young girl when she saw herself unable to hold him off any longer, 'right now, I have rather more on my mind than love; read the letter that has been sent to me, Monsieur: I am ruined.'

Whereupon she handed her husband a letter in which he read that the chateau of Téroze, four leagues away from the one in which the present scene is set, and situated in a corner of the forest of Fontainebleau where nobody ever goes, a dwelling whose revenue constituted his wife's dowry, had for six months been inhabited by ghosts that made a dreadful racket there, caused a nuisance to the tenant, spoiled the land and prevented both the President and his wife from ever picking up a penny from that estate unless they restored order there.

'That is dreadful news,' said the magistrate, handing back the letter, 'but could we not tell your father to give us something other than that nasty little chateau?'

'And what do you expect him to give us, Monsieur? Note that I am only a younger sister, he gave a great deal to my sister, it would be wrong of me to want to demand anything else; we must content ourselves with that and try to restore order there.'

'But your father knew about the problem when he married you off.'

'True, but he did not know all the details; in any case, that in no way diminishes the value of the gift, it merely postpones the benefit of it.'

'And does the Marquis know that?'

'Yes, but he does not dare to discuss it with you.'

'He is wrong not to do so; we must talk it over together.'

D'Olincourt was summoned; he could not deny the facts of the matter, and as a result they agreed that the simplest thing would be, whatever dangers might be involved, to go and live in that chateau for two or three days to bring those disorders to an end and see whether the married couple could not draw the revenue from it.

'Are you brave enough, President?' asked the Marquis.

'Me? It all depends,' said Fontanis. 'Courage is not a virtue that is especially relevant in our profession.'

'That I know,' said the Marquis. 'What you need most is fierceness, and the same pretty much goes for that virtue as for all the others – you have the art of stripping them so thoroughly of all their good qualities that only the aspects that spoil them are left.'

'I see: there you are again, sarcastic as ever, Marquis; let us talk sensibly, I beg you, and leave out the nasty remarks.'

'Well, it is time to leave, we must go and settle into Téroze, destroy the ghosts, sort out your lease and come back to sleep with your wife.'

'Wait, Monsieur, a moment, if you please, let us not head off quite so quickly; have you reflected on the dangers involved in going to share a house with people like that? The proper proceedings followed by a writ would be much better than any of that.'

'I see, there we have it: proceedings, writs… Why not excommunicate, the way priests do? Cruel weapons of tyranny and stupidity! When will all those hypocrites in skirts, all those pedantic fools in uniform, all those henchmen of Themis and Mary[36] stop believing that their insolent chattering and their inane bureaucracy can ever have any real effect on the world? Let me tell you, my brother, that it is not with scraps of paper such as those that you can make any impression on determined rascals; you need sabres, gunpowder and bullets. So you must resolve to die of hunger, or to pluck up the courage to confront them with those arms.'

'Monsieur le Marquis, you are discussing these things like a colonel of the dragoons; allow me to see things as a man of law whose person is sacred and dear to the State, and so cannot be exposed on any slight pretext.'

'Your person, dear to the State? I have not laughed for a long time, President, but I see you are intent on forcing that convulsion out of me. And how the devil, I ask you, could you ever imagine that a man commonly of low birth, an individual forever rebelling against all the good things his master desires, a character who serves that master neither with his purse nor with his person, ceaselessly obstructing his every good intention, and having but one thing in mind: fomenting division between individuals, maintaining the divisions of the kingdom, and causing distress to its citizens… I ask you, how can you imagine that such a creature can ever be of value to the State?'

'If you are going to lose your temper, I refuse to reply.'

'Well, my friend, in fact, I agree; I do indeed; even were you to reflect on this affair for a whole month, even if you were to get your Pantaloons[37] of colleagues to pronounce their comical opinions on the matter, I would still tell you that there is no other remedy in this case than to go and set up camp ourselves among the people who are trying to scare us.'

The President continued to try and wriggle out of it, putting forward a thousand paradoxes each more absurd and each more pompous and vain than the last, and finally concluded with the Marquis that he would set off the next day with him and two of the family's menservants. The President asked for La Brie to come with him; as we have said, we do not quite know why, but he had great confidence in that lad. D'Olincourt, all too aware of the important business that would keep La Brie in the chateau during this absence, replied that it would not be possible to take him too, and the next morning, at daybreak, they made their preparations for the journey. The ladies, who had got up early on purpose, dressed the President in an old suit of armour that they had found in the chateau; his young wife placed the helmet on his head, wishing him every success, and urged him to make a swift return so that he could receive from her hand the laurels that he would win. He embraced her tenderly, mounted his horse and followed the Marquis. Although they had made every effort to warn people in the neighbourhood of the masquerade that was about to pass by, the gaunt President clad in his military attire looked so completely ridiculous that he was followed from the one chateau to the other by roars of laughter and jeers. His only consolation was that the Colonel, who did not drop his serious mien for a single instant, would sometimes come up to him and say, 'As you can see, my friend, this world is nothing but a farce: we are sometimes the actor and sometimes the audience; either we judge what is happening on stage, or we appear on it.'

'True: but here they are hissing us,' the President kept saying.

'Do you think so?' the Marquis phlegmatically replied.

'There is little room for doubt,' replied Fontanis, 'and you have to admit, it is a hard thing to have to take.'

'Oh come now!' replied d'Olincourt. 'Are you and your kind not accustomed to these petty disasters, and do you imagine that, at each of the idiotic remarks you pass on your fleur-de-lis benches, the public does not also hiss you? You are naturally made to be mocked and scorned in your profession, as you wear grotesque costumes that make people laugh as soon as they set eyes on you; how can you imagine that with so many things telling against you on one side, you will be pardoned for your stupid comments on the other?'

'You are no friend to a judge's robes, Marquis.'

'I make no bones about the fact, President: I like only the occupations that are of some use. Any individual whose only talent is that of making up gods or killing off men thus strikes me as a person who deserves the anger of the public, and who should be either scoffed at or sentenced to hard labour. Do you think, my friend, that with the two excellent arms that nature has endowed you with, you would not be immeasurably better employed at a plough than in a law court? If you took up the first of these two occupations you would honour all the faculties you have received from heaven… In the second, you merely debase them.'

'But there must surely be judges.'

'It would surely be better if we just had virtues; these could be acquired without judges, and with judges, virtues are trampled underfoot.'

'And how do you expect a State to be governed…?'

'By three or four simple laws, recorded in the palace of the sovereign, and maintained in each social class by elders of that class: in this way, each social rank would have its peers, and if a gentleman were condemned, he would at least be spared the dreadful shame of being sentenced by low cads like you, so utterly worthless in comparison with him.'

'Oh! We will need to discuss that at much greater length…'

'The discussions will soon be over,' said the Marquis. 'Look, we have reached Téroze.'

And indeed they were already at the chateau. The tenant came to greet them, took their lordships' horses away, and they passed into a room where they were soon discussing with him the alarming events that had been taking place there.

Every evening, a dreadful noise echoed through every part of the house; no one could guess what was causing it. They had lain in wait and stayed up all night; several peasants employed by the tenant had, it was said, been beaten black and blue and nobody was eager to expose themselves to such a risk. But it was impossible to put their suspicions into words; the public rumour was merely that the spirit who kept coming back was that of a previous tenant of the household, who had been unjustly condemned to lose his life on the scaffold, and who had sworn that he would return every night to make a dreadful din in the house, until he had the satisfaction of wringing the neck of a magistrate.

'My dear Marquis,' said the President as he made for the door, 'it strikes me that my presence here is quite pointless; we are not accustomed to these kinds of vengeance and, like doctors, we want to be able to kill anyone we like, without fear or favour, without our victims being able to talk back at us after death.'

'One moment, my brother, one moment,' said d'Olincourt, holding back the President just as he was about to make his escape. 'Let us hear this man's account through the end.' Then he turned to the tenant and asked him, 'Is that all, Master

Pierre? Do you not have any further details about this singular turn of events, and is it all men of law to whom this hobgoblin is hostile?'

'No, Monsieur,' said Pierre. 'The other day he left a note on a table, in which he said that he was only against dishonest judges; any just judge runs no risks from him, but he will not spare those who, guided by nothing but despotism, stupidity or vengefulness, soon sacrifice their fellow human beings to their sordid passions.'

'Well, as you can see, it is time for me to withdraw,' said the President in consternation, 'my safety in this house really cannot be assured.'

'Ah, you villain!' said the Marquis, 'so your crimes are starting to make you tremble... You have destroyed people, eh? Sent them into exile for ten years merely for consorting with whores, vilely connived with families, received money for ruining a gentleman – and condemned so many other wretches to be sacrificed to your rage or ineptitude: these are the ghosts that haunt your imagination! Am I not right? How much would you give now to have been an honest man all your life! May this cruel situation be of some use to you one day, may you feel in advance how dreadfully remorse can weigh one down, and how there is not a single earthly happiness, of whatever value it may appear, that is worth the tranquillity of one's soul and the sweet pleasures of virtue.'

'My dear Marquis, I beg your pardon,' said the President with tears in his eyes, 'I am doomed, do not sacrifice me, I beg you, and let me return to your dear sister who is sorrowing over my absence and who will never forgive you for the ills to which you are about to deliver me.'

'Coward! How right people are when they say that poltroonery always goes with falseness and treachery... No, you will not escape, there is no drawing back, my sister has no dowry other than this chateau; if you wish to possess it, you must purge it of the rascals whose presence sullies it. Conquer or die: there is no alternative.'

'I beg your pardon, my dear brother, but there *is* an alternative: I could get out of here as fast as possible and give up my claim to possession.'

'Vile poltroon! So that is how you cherish my sister – you prefer to see her languishing in poverty than to fight to free her heritage… Do you want me to tell her on our return that those are the feelings you parade?'

'Good heavens, to what a dreadful state I am reduced!'

'Come now, let your courage return, and make yourself ready for what is expected of us.'

Their meal was served; the Marquis requested the President to dine in his full suit of armour; Master Pierre joined them in their meal; he said that until eleven in the evening there was absolutely nothing to fear, but that from that time until daybreak they would be quite unable to stay there.

'But stay here we will,' said the Marquis, 'and here is a brave comrade on whom I count as much as I do on myself. I am sure he will not abandon me.'

'Let us not make any rash promises,' said Fontanis. 'I must confess, I am rather like Caesar, my courage changes greatly from day to day.'[38]

Meanwhile, they spent the intervening time reconnoitring the environs, walking round, discussing affairs with the tenant, and when night fell, the Marquis, the President and their two servants shared out the chateau between them.

For his part, the President had a big room with two haunted towers on either side; the mere sight of the place made him shudder in anticipation: it was just here, they said, that the spirit would begin his rounds, so the President would soon have first-hand experience of him; a brave man would have revelled in this flattering hope, but the President, who, like all the presiding judges in the world (and in particular like those of Provence) was far from brave, allowed himself to give way to such a movement of trepidation on learning this, that they were obliged to give him a clean change of clothes, from head to foot; never had any medicine had a swifter effect. Anyway, they dressed and armed him again, placed two pistols on a table in his room, placed a lance at least fifteen feet long in his hands, lit three or four candles and abandoned him to his thoughts.

'O wretched Fontanis!' he exclaimed as soon as he was alone. 'What evil genie has led you into this mess? Could you not have found in your own province a girl who would certainly have been better than this one, and would not have caused you so much distress? It is all your fault, poor President, it is all your fault, my friend, here you are; a Parisian marriage tempted you, and now you can see the result... Crikey! Maybe you are going to die here like a dog, not even able to approach the sacraments or give up the ghost in the hands of a priest... Those damned unbelievers with their "equity", their "law of nature" and their "benevolence" – it seems as if paradise is obliged to open its gates to them once they have uttered those three words... Let us have less of nature, less of equity, less of benevolence: let us issue writs, let us exile, let us burn, let us break at the wheel, and let us go to mass – a much better way! This d'Olincourt, he is so utterly obsessed by the trial of that gentleman we passed sentence on last year; there must be some family or other link behind it, of which I was unaware... And yet, was it not a scandalous affair? Did not a thirteen-year-old manservant whom we had suborned come and tell us (since we had told him to tell us) that the man in question was killing whores in his chateau? Did he not come and regale us with a *Bluebeard's tale* that nurses would not dare to try and use even as a bedtime story? In a crime as important as the murder of a p—,[39] in a misdemeanour proven as demonstrably as the deposition for which we paid a child of thirteen (to whom we had given a hundred lashes since he would not say what we wanted him to say), it strikes me that one is not acting with undue severity if one proceeds in the way that we did… So do we need a hundred witnesses to prove a crime? Is it not enough to find an informer? And did our learned friends in Toulouse make such a close investigation when they had Calas broken at the wheel?[40] If we punished only the crimes we could prove, we would not enjoy the pleasure of dragging our fellow human beings to the scaffold so much as four times a century, and that is the only thing that makes us respected. I wish someone would tell me what kind of *parlement* it would be if its purse were always open to the needs of the State, if it never issued any remonstrances, if it registered all edicts and never killed anyone… It would be an assembly of fools that would not be taken in the least bit seriously by the rest of the nation… Be brave, President, be brave! You have merely done your duty, my friend: let the enemies of the magistracy clamour as they will, they will not destroy it; our power is built on the feebleness of kings, and it will last as long as the realm; may God grant the sovereigns that this power does not end up toppling them from the throne – though with a few more misfortunes such as those of the reign of Charles VII,[41] the monarchy will finally be destroyed, leading to that republican form of government that we have been promoting for so long, and which, placing us at the pinnacle of power like the Senate of

Venice, will at least deliver into our hands the chains with which we ardently long to crush the people.'

The President was mulling over these thoughts when a terrible noise echoed through all the rooms and down all the corridors of the chateau… His whole body started to shake, he clung to his chair, and hardly dare to raise his eyes. 'Fool that I am!' he cried. 'Should it be *my* task, the task of a member of the *Parlement* of Aix, to have to fight with spirits? Ah, spirits, what did you and the *Parlement* of Aix ever have to do with one another?' Meanwhile, the din grew louder, the doors to the two towers crashed open, and terrifying figures invaded the room… Fontanis fell to his knees, begged for mercy, implored them to spare his life.

'Villain!' one of the ghosts told him in a terrifying voice. 'Was pity ever in your heart when you unjustly condemned so many unfortunate people? Did their terrible fate ever move you? Did you ever become less vain, less proud, less greedy, less crapulous on the day when your unjust sentences plunged into misfortune or the grave the victims of your idiotic severity? And what gave rise to the dangerous impunity of your immediate power – that illusory force that mere opinion sustains for a brief moment and that philosophy straightaway destroys?… Allow us to act according to the same principles: yield, since you are the weaker.'

At these words, four of these bodily spirits laid strong hands on Fontanis, and in a twinkling stripped him as bare as your hand; all that came from him was tears, cries and a fetid sweat that covered him from head to foot.

'What shall we do with him now?' asked one of them.

'Wait,' said the one who seemed to be their leader, 'I have here the list of the four main murders that he juridically committed. Let us read it out to him:

'In 1750, he condemned to the wheel an unfortunate man whose only crime was to have refused to allow him to abuse his daughter.

'In 1754, he proposed that a man save his own life at the price of two thousand *écus*; when the man could not find this money, he had him hanged.

'In 1760, knowing that a man from his town had been talking about him, he condemned him the following year to be burnt as a sodomite, even though this unhappy man had a wife and a whole brood of children, all of which belied his crime.

'In 1772, a distinguished young man from his province tried to inflict a drubbing on a courtesan, as a playful vengeance for the nasty dose she had presented him with; that worthless clod turned the joke into a criminal affair, treating it as a case of murder and poisoning, and persuaded all his colleagues to go along with this ridiculous view; he destroyed the young man, ruined him and, when he could not lay hands on him, had him condemned to death for failing to appear in court.[42]

'These are his main crimes. You decide, my friends.'

Immediately, one voice shouted, 'An eye for an eye and a tooth for a tooth, Messieurs! He sentenced people unjustly to the wheel; I want him to be broken on the wheel in turn.'

'I vote for hanging,' said another, 'and for the same reasons as my colleague.'

'He will be burned,' said the third, 'both for having dared to use that form of execution unjustly, and for having frequently deserved it himself.'

'Let us give him an example of clemency and moderation, my comrades,' said the leader, 'and let us derive our sentence merely from his fourth adventure: thrashing a whore is a crime worthy of death in the eyes of this idiotic old fool; let him be given a thrashing himself.'

The unfortunate President was immediately seized and laid down flat on his stomach on a narrow bench, and tightly bound from head to foot; the four sprites each picked up a leather strap five feet long, and applied it rhythmically, with all the strength in their arms, to the exposed parts of the unhappy Fontanis's body. He, being hacked and cut for three solid quarters of an hour by the vigorous hands that had taken charge of his education, was soon nothing but a single wound, from which blood spurted out on all sides.

'That will do,' said the leader. 'As I said, let us be an example of pity and benevolence to him; if the rascal held *us* in his power, he would have us quartered; we are his masters, let us leave it at this fraternal chastisement, and let him learn from our school that it is not always by murdering men that one manages to make them better; he has merely been given five hundred lashes, and I will bet against all comers that this will cure him of his injustices, and that in future he will become one of the most just magistrates in his court; let him be untied, and we can continue with our operations.'

'Ouf!' exclaimed the President as soon as he had seen his tormentors depart. 'I can see that if we do shine a torch on the actions of others, if we try to expose them so as to enjoy the pleasure of punishing them, we are immediately paid back in the same coin. So whoever could have told those folk about all the things I have done, and however did they come to be so well informed about my behaviour?'

Either way, Fontanis managed to pull himself together as best he could, but hardly had he put his clothes back on than he heard dreadful screams from the direction the spirits had gone when they had left the room. He pricked up his ears, and recognised the voice of the Marquis calling for help at the top of his voice.

'The devil take me if I stir from here,' said the President, completely exhausted. 'Those rascals can give him a good drubbing as they did to me, if that is what they want; I am not getting involved, everyone has his own quarrels without becoming embroiled in those of others.'

However, the noise increased, and eventually d'Olincourt came into Fontanis's room, followed by his two menservants, all three of them screaming blue murder: they all three appeared to be covered with blood; one had his arm in a sling, another a bandage on his brow; and anyone who had seen them, all pale, dishevelled, and bloody as they were, would have sworn that they had just been fighting a legion of devils escaped from hell.

'Ah, my friend, what an attack!' cried d'Olincourt. 'I thought all three of us would be strangled.'

'I bet you have not been so badly mistreated as I have,' said the President, showing his bruised hind parts. 'Look at what they did to me!'

'Ah, my word, old friend,' said the Colonel, 'that immediately puts you in a strong position to lodge a fine and proper legal complaint; you know very well how intense an interest your colleagues have always taken, throughout the centuries, in whipped arses. Summon all the chambers together, my friend, find some famous lawyer prepared to exercise his eloquence in favour of your bruised and battered buttocks: resorting to the ingenious artifice by which an orator of ancient times was able to move the Areopagus by revealing to the eyes of the court the superb bosom of the beauty whom he was defending,[43] let your Demosthenes,[44] just as he is reaching the most pathetic moment of his speech, reveal those poignant buttocks and allow them to sway the audience to pity. Above all, remind the judges of Paris, before whom you will be obliged to appear, of that famous incident in 1769, when their hearts, much more compassionately moved by a tart's flogged behind than by the common people whose fathers they claim to be (and whom they nonetheless allow to die of starvation) – remind them of how they decided to put on trial a young soldier who, having just sacrificed his best years in the service of his prince, found that the only crown of laurels awaiting him on his return was the humiliation prepared by the worst enemies of the very same fatherland he had just been defending…[45] Come now, dear comrade in misfortune, let us make haste and be gone, there is no safety for us in this accursed chateau; let us swoop to our vengeance, let us rush to implore the equity of the protectors of public order, the defenders of the oppressed and the pillars of the State.'

'My legs will not support me,' said the President, 'and even if those wretched rascals were to peel me like an apple all over again, I beg you to have a bed provided for me, and leave me in peace and quiet for at least twenty-four hours.'

'Do not even think of it, my friend; you will be strangled.'

'Maybe, but it will merely be a just reward, and remorse is now awakening so powerfully in my heart that I will view as heaven's will all the misfortunes it will be pleased to send me.'

As the disturbances had completely finished, and d'Olincourt realised that the poor Provençal really did need a little rest, he summoned Master Pierre and asked him if they need fear those rascals returning that night.

'No, Monsieur,' replied the tenant, 'they will now stay quiet for eight to ten days and you can take your rest in complete safety.'

The President, almost unable to walk, was taken to a room where he went to bed and rested as well as he could for a good dozen hours or so; he was still lying there when he suddenly felt soaked in his bed; he looked up and saw that the ceiling had been pierced by a thousand holes, from each of which poured a fountain that risked flooding him if he did not decamp as fast as he could. He rushed down, completely naked, to the lower rooms, where he found the Colonel and Master Pierre drowning their sorrows over a pâté and a rampart of bottles of Burgundy wine. Their first response was to burst out laughing at the sight of Fontanis rushing into them in such indecent undress; he related his latest troubles to them, and they requested him to sit down at table, without giving him time to put on his trousers, which he was still holding over his arm in the manner of the peoples of Pegu[46]. The President started to drink, and found consolation for his woes at the bottom of the third bottle of wine; since they still had two hours more than were needed for their return to d'Olincourt, their horses were made ready, and they set off.

'That was a harsh lesson, Marquis, that you made me learn in your school,' said the Provençal as soon as he was in the saddle.

'It will not be the last, my friend,' replied d'Olincourt. 'Man is born to learn lessons – men of law in particular, for it is under an ermine robe that stupidity erected its temple, and only in your courts of law can it breathe freely. But anyway, whatever you might say, do you think we should have left that chateau without investigating what was going on there?'

'Are we any further forward now that we *do* know?'

'Certainly: now we can lodge our complaints with all the more reason.'

'Complaints? Devil take me if I lodge any complaints; I will keep what I already have for myself, and you will oblige me no end if you never mention it to anyone.'

'My friend, you are not being very logical. If it is absurd to lodge complaints when one is assailed, why did you unceasingly go round urgently begging others to lodge them? Ah, you are one of the greatest enemies of crime, and yet you are prepared to let it go unpunished when it has been witnessed so clearly? Is it not one of the most sublime axioms of jurisprudence that, even supposing the injured party abandons his claim, satisfaction is still owed to justice? Has not justice been visibly violated by what has just happened to you? And should you refuse to offer it the sacrifice that it legitimately demands?'

'As you will; but I will not speak a word of it.'

'What about your wife's dowry?'

'I will leave everything to the Baron's sense of equity, and I will merely charge him with the task of clearing up this business.'

'He will have nothing to do with it.'

'Very well, we will live on crusts.'

'What a brave fellow! You will cause your wife to curse you, and she will spend her life repenting that she ever yoked her fate to that of a poltroon such as you.'

'Oh, when it comes to remorse, we will each have our fair share of that, I believe. But why do you now want me to lodge a complaint, when you were so far from wishing so a while ago?'

'I did not know what was at stake. So long as I thought I could win without anyone's help, I chose this course as the most honest, and now that I find it essential to call the laws to our aid, it is what I propose that you do. So what is illogical about my behaviour?'

'Excellent, excellent,' said Fontanis, climbing down from his horse as they were arriving at d'Olincourt, 'but let us not breathe a word, I beg you; that is the one favour I would ask.'

Although they had been absent for only two days, things had been happening at the Marquise's. Mademoiselle de Téroze had taken to her bed; a supposed indisposition caused by the worry and anxiety of knowing that her husband was exposed to danger had kept her there for twenty-four hours, in an alluring bathing robe, with a thin veil twenty ells long wrapped round her head and neck... and a quite touching pallor, all of which made her a hundred times even more beautiful, and rekindled all the ardour of the President, especially as the whipping to which he had just been subjected inflamed his bodily senses even more. Delgatz was by the patient's bedside, and warned Fontanis in a low voice that he must not show the faintest sign of desire given the painful situation in which his wife found herself; the critical moment had arrived just as she was having her period; it was nothing less than a real uterine haemorrhage.

'Damn it all,' said the President, 'how unfortunate for me! I have just been given a thorough drubbing for the sake of this woman – a magisterial drubbing, indeed; and now I am deprived of the pleasure of receiving my recompense from her.'

In addition, the chateau now had another three visitors of whom we must give an account. Monsieur and Mme de Totteville, well-off people from the locality, had just brought along Mlle Lucile de Totteville, their daughter, a small, alert brunette of around eighteen, who was no whit less attractive than the languishing Mlle de Téroze. So as not to make the reader languish any longer, we will reveal straightaway the identity of these three new characters whom it had been found opportune to bring into the drama so as to postpone its denouement or conduct it more securely to the end proposed. Totteville was one of those ruined Knights of Saint-Louis[47] who went around dragging their order of chivalry through the mud in return for a few dinners or a few *écus*, accepting without demur all the roles that were devised for them to play; his supposed wife was an old adventuress of another kind who, finding that she was no longer of an age to traffic her physical charms, consoled herself by trading in the charms of others; as for the lovely princess who claimed kinship with them, one can easily guess – given the family of which she was a member – what class of person she came from. A student of Paphos[48] from childhood on, she had already been the ruin of two or three farmers general,[49] and it was because of her art and her allure that they had specially adopted her. However, each of these characters, chosen from the best of their class, distinguished in style, perfectly well educated, and possessing what is called the varnish of good tone, played the roles expected of them extremely well, and it was difficult, seeing them mingling with men and women of good company, not to believe that they too were part of it.

No sooner had the President arrived than the Marquise and her sister asked him for news of his adventure.

'It was nothing,' said the Marquis, as his brother-in-law had requested. 'It is a band of rascals that we will bring to heel sooner or later. We simply need to find out what the President's wishes on the matter may be; each of us will take pleasure in concurring with his views.'

And as d'Olincourt had quickly and privately informed them of what had happened, and of the President's desire that it be kept secret, they changed the subject and said no more about the ghosts of Téroze.

The President expressed his intense anxieties to his young wife, and even more the extreme distress it caused him that this cursed indisposition should force him to postpone yet again the instant of his happiness. And as it was late, that day they had supper and went to bed without anything untoward happening.

Monsieur de Fontanis who, as a good man of the robe, added to his other fine qualities that of being extremely attracted to the ladies, could not set eyes on young Lucile as she sat in the circle of the Marquise d'Olincourt without feeling a twinge of desire. He began by enquiring of his confident La Brie who this young lady might be, and when La Brie replied in such a manner as to foster the love that he could see being kindled in the magistrate's heart, the latter was persuaded to take things a step further.

'She is a girl of quality,' replied his cunning confidant, 'but she is not immune to a proposal of love from a man of your kind. Monsieur le Président,' continued the young rascal, 'you sow panic among fathers and terror among husbands, and however firmly an individual of the feminine gender might have resolved to behave herself, it is really difficult for one to resist you. Quite irrespective of your face, just think of your status: what woman can resist the attractions of a man of justice, that great black robe, that square bonnet... do you think all of that can fail to seduce?'

'It is indeed true that we are practically irresistible; we have a certain fellow at our beck and call who has always shed panic among the virtues... Anyway, La Brie, do you think that if I were to say a word...?'

'Surrender would follow, have no doubt.'

'But we would need to keep quiet about it – you must be aware that in my present situation, it is important for me not to start married life with an infidelity.'

'Oh, Monsieur, you would bring her to despair, she is so tenderly attached to you.'

'Yes – do you think she loves me a little?'

'She adores you, Monsieur, and it would kill her if you deceived her.'

'But do you think that, on the other side…?'

'Your affairs will make infallible progress if that is what you want; you have only to act.'

'Oh, my dear La Brie, that is music to my ears; what a pleasure to conduct two love affairs at once and deceive two women simultaneously! Deception, my friend, deception – what an intense pleasure for a man of law!'

In consequence of these encouragements, Fontanis smartened himself up, tidied his clothes, forgot all about the whipping that had left him cut and bruised, and, giving his wife (who remained in her bed) a cuddle, he directed his batteries at the cunning Lucile who, hearing him out with modesty at first, gradually started to play along with his suggestions.

This little game had been going on for about four days without anyone seeming to notice, when information from the gazettes and newspapers was received at the chateau, in which all astronomers were advised to observe that night *the passage of Venus under the sign of Capricorn.*

'Good Lord! That is a singular event,' said the President, like a connoisseur of such things, as soon as he had read this news. 'I would never have expected this phenomenon: as you are aware, Mesdames, I know a few things about this science, and I have even composed a work in six volumes on the *satellites of Mars.*'

'On the satellites of Mars?' said the Marquise with a smile. 'But they are not very favourable to you, President; I am surprised that you have chosen such a subject.'

'What a tease you are, charming Marquise! I see that my secret has been revealed; be that as it may, I am most curious to

59

see the event they are announcing… Do you happen to have any place here, Marquis, where we might go to observe the trajectory of this planet?'

'Certainly,' replied the Marquis. 'Do you not know that above my dovecot I have a fully equipped observatory? There you will find excellent telescopes, quadrants, compasses – in short, everything that comprises an astronomer's studio.'

'So you too are something of an astronomer!'

'Not at all, but one has eyes like everyone else; when we come across people who know about these things, we are all too happy to learn from them.'

'Well, it will be a pleasure for me to give you a few lessons; in six weeks I will teach you more about the Earth than Descartes or Copernicus ever knew.'

Meanwhile, the time to make their way to the observatory arrived; the President regretted that his wife's indisposition would deprive him of the pleasure of showing off his knowledge in front of her, without ever suspecting – poor devil – that it was she who was about to play the leading role in this singular performance.

Although balloons were not yet common, they were already known in 1779 and the skilful physicist who was going to perform the experiment we shall be describing, more knowledgeable than any of those who followed him, had the wit to express his admiration just like the others and not to breathe a word when intruders arrived to steal his discovery from him; in a perfectly constructed aerostat, at the prescribed time, Mlle de Téroze was to make an ascent in the arms of the Count d'Elbène, and this scene, viewed from a considerable distance and illuminated by nothing more than a gentle artificial flame, was cleverly enough arranged to impress a fool like the President, who had never in all his life read a single book about the science on which he prided himself.

The whole company came up to the top of the tower and equipped themselves with telescopes; the balloon set off.

'Can you see it?' everyone asked each other.

'Not yet.'

'Yes, I can see it!'

'No, that's not it.'

'I am sorry, on the left, on the left, turn the telescope to the east!'

'Ah, I have it!' exclaimed the President in the greatest delight, 'I have it, my friends, point your telescopes in the same direction as mine… A little closer than Mercury, not so far away as Mars, some way under the ellipsis of Saturn, there it is, ah, good Lord, what a wonderful sight!'

'I can see it as well as you, President,' said the Marquis, 'and it is indeed a superb thing. Can you make out the conjunction?'

'I have it right at the end of my telescope.'

At that moment the balloon passed right over the tower, and the Marquis said, 'Well now, were not the predictions that we read mistaken, and is that not *Venus over Capricorn*?'[50]

'Nothing could be more certain,' said the President. 'It is the most beautiful sight I have ever set eyes on.'

'Who knows?' said the Marquis. 'Maybe you will always be obliged to climb this high to see it at your ease?'

'Ah, Marquis, your jokes are out of place at such a wonderful time as this…'

And as the balloon drifted off into the darkness, everyone came down, delighted at the allegorical phenomenon with which art had just embellished nature.

'I really am sorry that you did not come to share with us the pleasure that we derived from this event,' said M. de Fontanis

61

to his wife, whom he found still in bed when he returned. 'Nothing finer could be seen.'

'I am sure you are right,' said the young woman, 'but I have been told that there were so many immodest things included in the spectacle that, to be quite honest, I am not in the least disappointed I did not see them.'

'Immodest?' said the President with a gracefully ironic smile… 'Oh, not at all, it was a conjunction: is there anything greater in nature? And a conjunction is what I would like to happen between the two of us, at long last, and happen it will, as soon as you want; but do tell me, in all conscience, sovereign mistress of my thoughts… Have you not made your slave languish long enough, and will you not soon grant him the reward for his sufferings?'

'Alas, my angel,' his young spouse lovingly told him, 'believe me when I tell you that I am as eager for it as you, if not more so, but you can see the condition I am in… and you see it without taking pity on it, cruel man, even though it is completely your doing: if you were less obsessed by your own desires, I would feel so much better.'

The President was in seventh heaven when he heard himself being teased like this; he strutted about and thrust his chest out; never did a man of the robe stick out his neck so far, not even one who has just hanged a man. But since, for all that, on Mlle de Téroze's side there were more and more obstacles in his way, while on Lucile's he was making excellent progress, Fontanis did not hesitate to prefer the blooming myrtles of love to the late-flowering roses of marriage. 'The one woman cannot escape me,' he kept telling himself. 'I can always have her whenever I want to, but the other may be here for just a short while; I must hasten to make the most of her presence.' Following these principles,

Fontanis did not waste any of the occasions that might further his plans.

'Alas, Monsieur,' the young woman said to him one day, with feigned innocence, 'will I not become the most unhappy of creatures if I grant you what you are demanding?… You are not free: will you ever be able to repair the damage you will do to my reputation?'

'What do you mean, "repair"? There is no "repairing" in a case such as this, neither of us will have to repair anything; it is merely what is called thrusting one's sword in the water. There is never anything to fear with a married man, since it is in his interest more than anyone's to keep the thing secret. So it will not stop you finding a husband of your own.'

'And what about religion, Monsieur, and honour…?'

'Do not talk of such depressing nonsense, my sweetheart, I can see clearly that you are a real Agnes[51] and need to spend some time in my school; ah! how I will dispel all those child-hood prejudices!'

'But I had thought that your profession obliged you to respect them?'

'Yes, that is true – on the outside: we have only outer appearances for us, so we need to make an impression on the outside at least, but once we are stripped of that vain decorum that obliges us to show respect, we are just like the rest of mortals. Ah, how could you possibly imagine we are free of their vices? Our passions are much more inflamed by the story (or the depiction) of theirs, and do not draw any distinction between them and us apart from the excesses that they fail to recognise and that comprise our daily delights; almost always sheltered from the laws with which we make other people tremble, this impunity inflames us and simply makes us even more wicked…'

Lucile listened to all of these trifling comments, and however much horror she felt for both the body and mind of this abominable character, she continued to entice him along, since the reward that she had been promised came only on these conditions. The more amorous the President became, the more his fatuousness made him intolerable: there is nothing in the world as comical as a lawyer in love – he is the perfect picture of gaucheness, impertinence and ineptitude. If the reader has even see a cock about to propagate his species, he will have, from the sketch with which we are presenting him, the most complete idea. Whatever precautions he took to disguise his plans, one day, his insolence of manner revealed them just a little too clearly, and the Marquis decided to challenge him at table, and humiliate him in front of his goddess.

'President,' he told him, 'I have this very instant received some rather distressing news for you.'

'How is that?'

'I am reliably informed that the *Parlement* of Aix is to be abolished; the public complains that it is useless, Aix has much less need of a *parlement* than does Lyons, and this latter city, much too far from Paris to be dependent on it, will include the whole of Provence; it dominates the region, and is altogether well placed to harbour within in its walls the judges of such a major province.'

'This arrangement is not at all sensible.'

'Oh but it is. Aix is at the other end of the world; whichever part of the province a Provençal may live in, he would always prefer to go to Lyons for his affairs than to that pigsty of yours known as Aix. The roads are dreadful, and there is no bridge over the Durand which, like you, quite loses its head for nine months of the year. And then there are, I am bound to say,

64

more particular failings laid at your door: firstly, they criticise those who comprise your body, saying that in the whole *Parlement* of Aix there is not a single person of note... just tuna merchants, sailors, smugglers, in a word a horde of contemptible rascals with whom the nobility refuses to have anything to do and who persecute the people to avenge themselves for the discredit into which they have fallen, a pack of fools and imbeciles... Forgive me, President, I am merely relating what I have read; I will give you the letter to peruse after dinner. In a word, they are scoundrels who take fanaticism and scandal so far that, as proof of their integrity, they leave, always ready and waiting in the town centre, a scaffold, which is nothing but a monument to their mean-spirited severity. The people ought to tear the stones from it and hurl them at the vile tormentors who so insolently dare to offer them nothing but chains. It is amazing that they have not done so yet, and there is a rumour that it will happen soon... A host of unjust legal decisions, an affectation of severity whose object is to enable them to indulge in all the legislative crimes they are pleased to commit, and there are even more serious offences than these... They are definitely the enemies of the State, and will be viewed as such for ever and ever – people are daring to say so openly. The public horror that your execrations of Mérindol inspired has still not faded from every heart; did you not at that time present the most horrible spectacle one can possibly depict? Can one imagine without a shudder those guardians of order, peace and equity running through the province like madmen, holding a torch in one hand and a sword in the other, burning, killing, massacring all before them, like a herd of crazed tigers that had escaped from the woods? Should magistrates really behave in such a fashion? People also recall several circumstances in which you stubbornly refused to help the King when he needed it, and several times you were ready to bring the province into open revolt rather than to allow yourselves to be involved in tax-collecting.[52] Do you think people have forgotten that unhappy period, when, despite the fact that no danger threatened, you came at the head of the citizens of your town to hand over its keys to the Constable of Bourbon who was betraying his king?[53] Or the time when, trembling at the mere approach of Charles V, you hastened to pay him homage and to allow him into your walls? Everyone must know that it was in the *Parlement* of Aix that the first stirrings of the League were fomented.[54] In a word, have you at all times been anything other than sedition-mongers or rebels, murderers or traitors? You know this better than anyone, Messieurs, you magistrates of Provence: when a man seeks the downfall of another, he finds out everything he has done in the past, he takes care to remind people of all his former misdeeds so as to add them to the more recent ones: so do not be at all surprised if people treat you the same way that you treated the unfortunates whom it pleased you to sacrifice to your pedantic zeal; let me tell you, dear President, it is not permitted to an institution any more than it is to an individual to insult an honest and peaceable citizen, and if this institution takes it into its head to commit such a folly, it has no reason to be surprised if the voices of all men are raised against it to proclaim the rights of the weak and virtuous against despotism and iniquity.

Since the President could neither tolerate these accusations, nor reply to them, he rose from table like a man possessed, swearing that he would leave the house forthwith. After the sight of a man of the robe in love, there is nothing quite so risible as one who is beside himself with anger: the muscles of his face are naturally disposed to hypocrisy, and when they are obliged to pass suddenly from hypocrisy to the contortions of rage, they can do so only by moving through violent transitions whose progress is comical to see. When they had all enjoyed his temper tantrum, and since they had not yet reached the scene that, they hoped, would rid them of him once and for all, they made an effort to calm him down; they ran after him and brought him back, and Fontanis found it relatively easy to forgive that evening all the petty vexations he had suffered in the morning, reassumed his usual demeanour, and the whole business was forgotten.

Mademoiselle de Téroze was feeling better, although she still looked rather pale and tired; she came down to meals and even went for walks with the others. The President, less impatient now that he was entirely preoccupied by Lucile, saw that he would, nonetheless, soon have to turn all of his attentions to his wife. Consequently, he decided to hasten along his other affair, which had reached the critical moment: Mlle de Totteville had ceased to make any objections, and all he needed was to find a safe place for their assignation. The President suggested his bachelor apartment; Lucile did not sleep in her parents' room and so was happy to accept this as the setting for that night's meeting, and immediately informed the Marquis. The part she was to play was outlined to her, and the rest of the day went off peaceably. At around eleven, Lucile, who was to get into the President's bed first thanks to a key to his room that he secretly gave her, claimed she had a headache and went out. A quarter of an hour later, the impatient Fontanis also withdrew, but the Marquise told him that on this particular evening she wished to do him the honour of accompanying him to his room. Everyone present played along, and Mlle de Téroze was the first to enjoy the joke. Without paying any regard to the President, who was like a cat on hot bricks, and would have been all too glad either to escape from this ridiculous politeness or at least to forewarn the woman whom he imagined would be caught by surprise, they all picked up a candle; the men went through first, the women surrounded Fontanis, they held him by the hand, and this merry procession made its way to the door of his bedroom... Our unfortunate gallant could hardly breathe.

'I have no idea how this will turn out,' he stammered. 'Think how incautiously you are behaving! Who says that the object of my affections is not awaiting me this very instant in my bed? And if that is the case, just think of all that may result from your irresponsible behaviour!'

'At all events,' said the Marquise, suddenly pushing open the door, 'come now, beauty! It appears that you are waiting for the President in bed. Show yourself! Do not be afraid!'

But great was the surprise of all when the candles shone onto the bed and revealed a monstrous donkey lolling on the sheets! By a comical twist of fate, the donkey, doubtless delighted at the role he had been given to play, had peacefully gone to sleep on the magistrate's bed and was snoring voluptuously.

'Oh! Good Lord!' exclaimed d'Olincourt, holding his sides with laughter. 'Just look, President, at how that animal is lying there, calm and cool as you like! Does he not resemble one of your colleagues at a hearing?'

The President, however, was only too happy to have got off with this joke. He imagined he would be able to draw a veil over the rest, and that Lucile, having learnt of this turn of events, would have had the good sense not to arouse any suspicions about their intrigue. So the President started to laugh along with the others. They extricated the donkey as well as they could (he was most displeased at having his sleep interrupted), put clean sheets on the bed, and Fontanis took the place – quite fittingly – of the most superb donkey they had ever seen in that part of the world.

'Honestly, you cannot tell them apart,' said the Marquise when she had seen him go to bed. 'I would never have believed there was such a complete resemblance between a donkey and a President of the *Parlement* of Aix.'

'How mistaken you were, Madame!' replied the Marquis. 'Did you not know that is from among learned creatures such as this that the law court of Aix has always selected its members? I bet that the one you have just seen leaving was its very first president.'

The next morning, Fontanis's first thought was to ask Lucile how she had managed to evade detection. She knew her lines well and told him that she had learnt of the joke and quickly slipped away, but she had been worried that she had, none-theless, been betrayed, and this had meant she had spent a dreadful night, and longed most ardently for the moment when she would be given an explanation. The President reassured her and obtained from her a promise that she would meet with him the next day. Lucile coyly offered a little resistance, which merely fanned the flames of Fontanis's ardour, so that every-thing was arranged as he desired. But if this first assignation had been ruined by a comic joke, imagine what a fateful event was about to forestall the second! The same arrangements were made as the day before. Lucile withdrew the first, and the President followed her shortly afterwards without anyone stopping him. He found her in the meeting place they had arranged, clasped her in his arms, and was already on the point of giving her quite unequivocal proof of his passion…. when all of a sudden the doors opened, and in came M. and Mme de Totteville, the Marquise and Mlle de Téroze herself.

'Monster!' exclaimed the latter, flinging herself in a fury at her husband. 'Is this the way you make sport of my innocence and my affection?'

'Horrid daughter!' said M. de Totteville to Lucile, who had fallen to her knees at her father's feet. 'So this is how you abuse the liberty we innocently granted you!…'

For their part, the Marquise and Mme de Totteville stared wrathfully at the guilty pair, and Mme d'Olincourt's mind was diverted from this initial reaction only to catch her sister as she fainted away in her arms. It would be difficult to depict Fontanis's expression in the midst of this scene: surprise, shame, terror, anxiety – all these different emotions swept through him at once, and made him stand there as motionless as a statue. In the meantime, the Marquis arrived, enquired what had happened, and was filled with indignation when they told him.

'Monsieur,' Lucile's father said to him firmly, 'I would never have expected that, in your house, an honourable young woman might have to fear affronts of this kind; you will understand me if I tell you that I will not tolerate it, and that my wife, my daughter and I are leaving straightaway to demand justice from those of whom we may expect it.'

'Truly, Monsieur,' the Marquis then said coldly to the President, 'you have to agree that these are scenes I could hardly have expected. So was it merely in order that you might dishonour my sister-in-law and my family that it has pleased you to ally yourself with us?'

Then, turning to Totteville, he said, 'There is nothing more just than the reparation you are demanding, but may I make so bold as to ask you forthwith to avoid any scandal? It is not for that wretch there that I ask it, since he deserves nothing but contempt and punishment – it is for myself, Monsieur, for my family, and for my unhappy father-in-law who, having placed all his trust in this Pantaloon, will die of grief at the way he has been deceived.'

'I would be glad to oblige you, Monsieur,' said M. de Totteville haughtily, as he led his wife and his daughter away, 'but you will allow me to place my honour higher than these considerations; you will in no wise be compromised, Monsieur, in the charges I shall be bringing; that dishonest wretch alone will be implicated… Forgive me if I refuse to hear any more, and that I go henceforth to a place where I can prepare my revenge.'

On these words, these three characters withdrew, as no human effort could have stopped them, and hastened – as they had said – to Paris, to lodge a complaint with the *Parlement* against the indignities that the Président de Fontanis had tried to heap on them… In the mean time, this unhappy chateau was filled with dismay and despair; Mlle de Téroze, who had barely recovered from her previous illness, took to her bed again with a fever that was, they took care to proclaim, highly dangerous. Monsieur and Mme de Fontanis fulminated against the President, who, in the extremity that now threatened him, had nowhere to take refuge outside this house and so did not dare to protest against the reprimands that were so justly addressed to him; and things remained in this state for three days, when finally the Marquis was secretly informed that the affair was being treated extremely seriously as a criminal matter, and that Fontanis was about to be proscribed.

'What? Without giving me a hearing?' said the President in the greatest alarm.

'Is that the rule?' asked d'Olincourt. 'Are means of defence permitted to the man proscribed by law? Is it not rather one of your respectable customs that you condemn him without hearing his side of the story? Only the weapons that you have used against others are here being employed against you; after exercising injustice for thirty years, is it not reasonable that you should fall victim to it just once in your life?'

'But just for a few women?'

'A few women? What do you mean? Do you not know that affairs of such a kind are the most dangerous? What was that unhappy business, the memory of which earned you five hundred lashes in the ghost-haunted chateau, if not an "affair of women", and did you not think it was permissible to ruin a gentleman's good name all over an "affair of women"? An eye for an eye and a tooth for a tooth, President, that is your moral compass, so bravely set your bearings by that.'

'Good heavens,' said Fontanis, 'in God's name, my brother, do not abandon me.'

'Do you think that we will help you,' replied d'Olincourt, 'whatever dishonour you have brought down on us, and whatever cause for complaint against you we may have? But the means are hard… You know what they are.'

'What are they?'

'The King's favour, a *lettre de cachet*:[55] that seems to me the only way.'

'What dreadful and extreme measures!'

'I agree; but what others can you find? Do you wish to leave France and ruin yourself for good, when a few years in prison might well settle all this? Besides, although this is a solution that revolts you, is it not one that you and your kind have sometimes used? Was it not by recommending this barbarous means that you succeeded in crushing that gentleman whom the spirits have so thoroughly avenged? Did you not, in a case of maladministration as dangerous as it was punishable, force that unhappy soldier to choose between prison and disgrace, and hold back the thunderbolts of your contemptible wrath only on condition that he would be crushed by those of his king? And so, my friend, there is nothing in my suggestions that should come as a surprise; not only is this course of action well known to you, it is now, indeed, one that you should welcome.'

'Ah, dreadful memories!' said the President, shedding tears. 'Who would have told me that heaven's vengeance would break on my head at almost the very instant when my crimes were being committed? What I have done is here repaid: let us suffer and hold our peace.'

However, since help was urgently required, the Marquise urged her husband to set off for Fontainebleau, where the court was in residence. As for Mlle de Téroze, she did not take any part in this discussion; shame and grief in appearance, and the Count d'Elbène in reality, kept her in her bedroom, whose door was firmly closed against the President; he had presented himself there several times, and had tried to use his tears and remorse to open it, but always in vain.

So the Marquis left; his journey was a short one, and he arrived back two days later, escorted by two officers of the watch, and armed with what looked like an order. As soon as he set his eyes on it, the President started to tremble in every limb.

'You could not have arrived at a better time,' said the Marquise, pretending that she had received news from Paris while her husband was at court. 'The trial is proceeding with extraordinary speed, and my friends have written to tell us to get the President away as soon as possible; my father has been alerted, he is in despair, he urges us to give his friend a helping hand, and describes the grief into which all of this has plunged him… His health means that the only help he can offer is that of his good wishes, which would be more sincere if Fontanis had been a wiser man… Here is the letter.'

The Marquis hastily read it, and after haranguing Fontanis, who was finding it very difficult to reconcile himself to the idea of prison, he handed him over to his two guards, who were in fact two quartermasters from his own regiment, and exhorted him to console himself with the thought that he would not forget him.

'I have, with great difficulty, managed to get you a chateau situated some five or six leagues from here,' he told him. 'There you will be under the orders of an old friend of mine who will treat you the same way he would treat myself. I have given your guards a letter for him in which I commend you to him even more strongly, so you can rest assured.'

The President wept like a child; there is nothing so bitter as remorse at a crime when the criminal sees all the torments he has himself used against others falling on his own head… But he had no choice but to tear himself away. He insistently requested permission to embrace his wife.

'Your wife?' the Marquise said to him brusquely. 'Luckily she is not yet your wife, and this is the only thing that softens the blow of all the calamities that have befallen us.'

'Very well,' said the President, 'I will be brave enough to sustain this wound as well,' and he climbed into the officers' carriage.

The chateau to which this unfortunate man was led was on an estate belonging to the dowry of Mme d'Olincourt, where all had been made ready for his arrival; a captain in d'Olincourt's regiment, a sour, surly man, was to play the role of governor. He received Fontanis, dismissed the guards, and harshly informed his prisoner, as he sent him off to a very mean room, that he had been given further orders of a severity that he could not ignore. The President was left in this cruel situation for nearly a month; nobody came to see him, he was given nothing but soup, bread and water, he had to sleep on straw in a dreadfully damp room, and people only ever came into his room the same way as visitors in the Bastille – in other words like those who come into a menagerie, just to feed the animals. The unfortunate man of the robe was cruelly tormented by his own thoughts during his stay in this dismal abode; nothing came to distract him; finally the false governor appeared and after giving him some ineffectual consolation he spoke to him as follows.

'You can be in no doubt, Monsieur, that the first of your misdeeds was to wish to marry into a family that is so superior to you in every respect; the Baron de Téroze and the Count d'Olincourt are men of the highest nobility, known throughout the whole of France, and you are nothing but a wretched provincial magistrate, without name or influence, status or prestige. So the slightest reflection on your own position should have obliged you to show the Baron de Téroze, who was unaware of your real rank, that you were not in the least suited to his daughter; how, in any case, could you believe for a moment that this girl, as beautiful as love itself, could ever become the wife of a disgusting old monkey like you? One can be mistaken about oneself, but not to such a point, Monsieur. The thoughts that must have been going through your mind during your stay here, Monsieur, must have convinced you that throughout the four months during which you were stay-ing in the house of the Marquis d'Olincourt, you were nothing but an object of scorn and derision. Men of your rank and bearing, your profession and stupidity, your wickedness and treachery, cannot expect anything other than treatment of that kind. By a thousand tricks, each more comical than the last, you were prevented from enjoying the woman to whose land you laid claim; you were given five hundred lashes in a ghost-haunted castle, you were shown your wife in the arms of the man she adores – which you idiotically took for a natural phenomenon – you were embroiled with a whore, hired for the occasion, who made a complete fool of you; in short, you have been locked away in this chateau, and it is entirely up to the Marquis d'Olincourt, my colonel, whether he keeps you here for the rest of your life, which will most certainly be the case if you refuse to sign this paper. Observe, before you read it, Monsieur,' continued the false governor, 'that society views you merely as a man who was engaged to marry Mademoiselle de Téroze, but not in the least as her husband; your wedding was celebrated in the greatest secrecy, and the few witnesses to it have agreed to say nothing of it; the priest has handed over the marriage licence, here it is; the notary has returned the contract, you can see it with your own eyes. Furthermore, you have never slept with your wife, so your marriage is null and void; thus it is tacitly annulled with the full consent of all parties, which rescinds it as definitively as if it had been broken off by the full force of civil and religious laws. Here, likewise, the Baron of Téroze and his daughter attest that they have withdrawn from the arrangements; you need only to agree to do likewise; here is the paper, Monsieur, choose between signing it of your own free will and the certainty that you will spend the rest of your days here… I have spoken. What is your answer?'

The President reflected for a while, then took the paper and read these words:

'I attest to all who will read these presents that I have never been the husband of Mademoiselle de Téroze; I hereby restore to her all the rights over her which for a while it was purposed to grant me, and I promise that will never lay claim to them again during my lifetime. Furthermore, I can have nothing but praise for the way she and her family treated me during the summer I spent in their house; it is of one accord, and of our own free will, that we both mutually renounce the planned union that had been arranged for us, that we restore to each other reciprocally the liberty to dispose of our persons just as if there had never been any intention of joining us together. And it is in full liberty of body and mind that I sign this, in the chateau of Valnord, the property of Madame la Marquise d'Olincourt.'

'You told me, Monsieur,' replied the President once he had read these lines, 'what awaited me if I did not sign, but you have not made any mention of what would happen to me if I agreed to everything.'

'You will instantly be rewarded with your freedom, Monsieur,' replied the false governor, 'together with a request to accept this piece of jewellery, worth two hundred louis, from Madame la Marquise d'Olincourt, and the certainty that you will find, at the gate of the chateau, your manservant and two excellent horses waiting to take you back to Aix.'

'I will sign and depart, Monsieur; I am so eager to escape from the clutches of all these people that I will not hesitate for a single moment.'

'So, all is well, President,' said the Captain, taking the signed paper and handing over the jewel. 'But take care that you behave; once you are out of here, if any foolish desire for vengeance should at any time overcome you, just remember, before you act upon it, that you have a mighty adversary, that this powerful family (all of whose members you would offend by your actions) would immediately have you declared mad, and the asylum set apart for those unfortunates would forever become your final dwelling place.'

'Fear nothing, Monsieur,' said the President, 'it is in my interest more than anyone's not to wish to get involved with such people ever again; I promise I will keep my distance from them.'

'That is what I advise you, President,' said the Captain, finally opening his prison door. 'Depart in peace and never be seen again in this part of the world.'

'You have my word on it,' said the man of the robe, as he mounted his horse. 'This little adventure has cured me of all my vices. Even if I were to live for another thousand years, I would never come looking for a wife in Paris; I had sometimes guessed at the sorrow one must feel on being cuckolded after marriage, but I had no idea that it was possible to be cuckolded before… I will show the same wisdom and discretion in my sentences, I will never again set myself up as a mediator between women and men who are better than me – it costs too much to take the part of those little ladies, and I no longer wish to have anything to do with men who have ghostly spirits all ready and waiting to avenge them.'

The President disappeared; he became wise after the event, and no one heard any more of him. The whores complained, as there was no one left in Provence to stand up for them, and morality gained thereby, since young women, finding themselves deprived of their immoral supporter, now preferred the path of virtue to the dangers that might well await them on the path of vice, since magistrates were now wise enough to sense the dreadful problems that any attempt to protect them might entail.

As the reader can imagine, during the President's detention, the Marquis d'Olincourt persuaded the Baron de Téroze that he had been mistaken to hold his excessively favourable opinion of Fontanis, and took pains to ensure that all the arrangements we have just seen were safely put into effect; his skill and influence carried the thing off so well that three months afterwards, Mlle de Téroze married the Count d'Elbène in a public ceremony, and lived with him happily ever after.

'I sometimes regret having mistreated that villain so badly,' the Marquis said to his sister-in-law one day. 'But when, on the one hand, I consider the happiness that has resulted from my actions, and on the other hand persuade myself that I merely persecuted a buffoon who was of no use to society, and at bottom an enemy of the State, a disturber of the public peace, the tormentor of an honest and respectable family, and the signal defamer of a gentleman whom I esteem and to whom I have the honour of being linked, I console myself and exclaim with the philosopher,[56] "O sovereign Providence, why are men's means so limited that the only way they can ever contrive to do good is by doing a little evil!"'

Finished this story on 16th July 1787 at 10 p.m.

Émilie de Tourville
or
Brotherly Cruelty

There is nothing so sacred in a family as the honour of its members, and yet if this treasure is ever tarnished – however precious it may be – should those responsible for defending it go so far as to assume the humiliating role of persecutors of the unhappy creatures who cause them offence? Would it not be reasonable to weigh in the balance the horrors they visit on their victims with the often imaginary wrong they complain has been done to them? After all, who is guiltier in the eyes of reason: a weak and deceived girl, or some relative or other who, by setting up as a family's avenger, becomes the tormentor of the hapless creature? The incidents we are about to present to our reader will perhaps answer the question.

The Count de Luxeuil, a lieutenant-general some fifty-six to fifty-seven years old, was travelling home in a post-chaise from one of his estates in Picardy when, passing through the forest of Compiègne, at around six o'clock one evening towards the end of November, he heard a woman's cries that seemed to be coming from a bend in one of the roads that ran near the highway that he was travelling down; he stopped, and ordered his manservant, who was running alongside his post-chaise, to go and see what the problem was. He was told that it was a young girl of sixteen to seventeen, covered from head to foot in her own blood, though it was impossible to make out where she had been wounded; she was calling for help. The Count immediately climbed out and rushed over to the poor girl; in the darkness, he too found it difficult to see where the blood she was losing could be coming from, but her replies to his questions eventually led his eye to the vein of the arm where a patient is usually bled.

'Mademoiselle,' said the Count, after giving this creature all the help he could, 'I am in no position to ask you what has caused your distress, nor are you really in a fit state to tell me; climb into my carriage, I beg you, and let us direct our efforts, you to calming yourself down, and I to assisting you.'

With these words, Monsieur de Luxeuil, assisted by his manservant, carried that poor young lady into his post-chaise, and they set off.

No sooner did this attractive girl realise that she was now safe than she tried to stammer out a few words of thanks, but the Count begged her not to speak, and told her, 'Tomorrow, Mademoiselle, you will tell me, I hope, everything about yourself, but today, thanks to the authority over you that falls to me because of my age and my great good fortune in being able to help you, I must insist that you concentrate on calming yourself down.'

They reached their destination; to avoid any fuss, the Count wrapped his protégée in a man's cloak and had her taken by his manservant to a comfortable apartment at the far end of his residence, where he came to see her as soon as he had been lovingly greeted by his wife and son who had been expecting him for supper that evening.

When the Count came to see his patient, he brought a surgeon with him. The young woman was examined and was found to be in an indescribable state of prostration: the pallor of her complexion seemed to indicate that she had only a few moments left to live, and yet she was not wounded; as for her weakness, it was the result, so she said, of the huge quantity of blood that she had been losing every day for the last three months, and as she was just about to tell the Count what extraordinary cause lay behind such an amazing loss of blood, she fell into a swoon, and the surgeon declared that she needed to be left in peace and quiet; they should do no more than administer restoratives and cordials to her.

Our unfortunate young woman spent a relatively comfortable night, but for six days she was in no state to inform her benefactor of the events that had befallen her; finally, on the seventh evening, while everyone else in the Count's house remained unaware that she was there, and as she herself, thanks to the precautions he had taken, also had no idea where she was, she begged the Count to hear her out and in particular to grant her his indulgence, whatever the misdemeanours to which she was about to confess. Monsieur de Luxeuil pulled up a chair, assured his protégée that he would never deprive her of the concern that she naturally aroused in him, and our lovely adventuress thereupon embarked on the tale of her woes.

The story of Mademoiselle de Tourville

I am, Monsieur – she said – the daughter of the Président de Tourville, a man too well known and eminent in status for you not to know of him. In the two years since I left the convent, I have never left my father's home; since I lost my mother while still very young, he alone took care of my upbringing, and I can say that he spared no effort to give me all the graces and accomplishments of my sex. This attentiveness, and the plans my father announced of having me make the best possible marriage as soon as possible, and maybe even a certain preference he showed for me – all of these things soon aroused the jealousy of my brothers, one of whom, who was appointed a magistrate three years ago, has just reached his twenty-sixth year and the other of whom, who has more recently been made a councillor, will soon be twenty-four.

I never imagined I could be so fiercely hated by them as I am now convinced I was; having done nothing to deserve these feelings on their part, I lived in the sweet illusion that they felt the same way for me as, in my heart's innocence, I did for them. Ah, good heavens, how wrong I was! Except for the times when my education was taken in hand, I enjoyed the greatest freedom in my father's house; he left me to behave as I saw fit, and placed no restrictions on me; indeed, for almost eighteen months I had been given permission to walk with my maid every morning either on the terrace of the Tuileries, or on the rampart near where we live, and likewise to pay a visit in her company, either on foot or in one of my father's carriages, to one of my female friends or relations, so long as this was not at a time of day when a young woman can hardly be left alone in the middle of a circle of other people. This ill-fated freedom was the sole cause of my misfortunes, and that is why I am telling you of it, Monsieur – I wish to God I had never been granted it!

One year ago, as I was out walking, as I have just said, with my maid (whose name is Julie), down a dim and shady path in the Tuileries, where I felt less exposed to public view than on the terraces, and where I seemed to breathe a purer air, six ill-disciplined young men accosted us, and demonstrated, through the indecency of their comments, that they took both of us to be what are called 'whores'. Dreadfully embarrassed by such a scene, and not knowing which way to turn, I was just about to take flight to a place of greater safety when a young man whom I very often used to see out walking at about the same time of day as myself, and whose appearance seemed to betoken that he was a thoroughly decent person, happened to come by just as I was in this cruel quandary.

'Monsieur!' I cried, summoning him over, 'I do not have the honour to be known to you, but we cross each other's paths here almost every morning; what you may have seen of me must have convinced you – I sincerely hope – that I am not an opportunistic young woman; I urgently beg you to give me your hand and take me back home, and to deliver me from these bandits.'

Monsieur de — (if you do not mind, I will not mention his name, since I have every good reason not to do so) immediately came running over, and sent the rascals gathered round me packing. He convinced them they were mistaken by showing me every politeness and respect, and he took me by the arm and straightaway led me from the garden.

'Mademoiselle,' he said, just before we reached the door of my house, 'I think it better to leave you here; if I take you all the way home, we will have to explain why; perhaps this will lead to your being forbidden to go out walking by yourself alone; so make no mention of what has just happened, and continue to come to the same pathway as usual, since you enjoy doing so and your parents permit it. I will not fail to be there every single day and you will always find me ready to give my life, if need be, to prevent anyone disturbing your peace and quiet.'

A wise precaution of this kind, and such an obliging offer, made me gaze at this young man with somewhat greater interest than I had felt like doing until then; finding that he was two or three years older than myself and had a charming face, I blushed as I thanked him, and the flaming arrows of that seductive deity who is the cause of my present misfortunes pierced my heart before I had any time to shield myself from them. We went our ways, but I thought I could tell, from the manner in which M. de — left me, that I had made the same impression on him as he had just produced on me. I went back to my father's home, I refrained from mentioning the incident, and returned the next day to the same avenue, led there by a feeling stronger than myself, which would have made me defy all dangers that one might meet with there… Indeed, perhaps I might even have desired them, just for the pleasure of being delivered by the same man… I am portraying my soul to you, Monsieur, with perhaps a little too much naivety, but you promised to be indulgent and every new detail in my story will show you just how much I need it; this is not the only act of imprudence that you will be seeing me commit, and this is not the only time I will be in need of your pity.

Monsieur de — appeared in the avenue six minutes after me, and as soon as he saw me came up to me and said, 'May I make so bold, Mademoiselle, as to enquire whether yesterday's incident has caused any stir, and whether it has caused you any inconvenience?'

I reassured him, and told him that I had followed his advice, for which I thanked him, and sincerely hoped that nothing would now spoil the pleasure I took in coming here to enjoy the morning air.

'If you find this place has its charms, Mademoiselle,' replied M. de — most politely, 'I am sure that those who have the good fortune to meet you here experience a charm even more intense, and if I took the liberty of advising you yesterday not to risk doing anything that might interrupt your walks, the truth is that you owe me no thanks: I have to tell you, Mademoiselle, that I did what I did less for you than for myself.'

And his eyes, as he said these words, turned to mine with such expression… oh, Monsieur, to think that it was to this tender man that I would one day owe my misfortunes! I replied politely to his remarks, and we struck up a conversation; we walked along together for a while and M. de — made a point, before leaving me, of imploring me to tell him the name of the person to whom he had been fortunate enough to render a service the previous day; I did not feel obliged to conceal my name from him, and he in turn told me who he was; whereupon we parted. And so, for nearly a month, Monsieur, we did not stop seeing each other almost every day, and this month, as you will easily imagine, did not go by without our admitting to our feelings for one another, and without our swearing that we would never cease to harbour them.

Finally, M. de — begged me to allow him to see me in a less public place than this park.

'I do not dare to present myself at your father's, my lovely Émilie,' he told me. 'As I have never had the honour to know him, he would soon guess at the reason that was impelling me to visit his home, and instead of this action helping our plans along, it might in fact greatly hinder them, but if indeed you are kind enough and compassionate enough not to want me to die of the sorrow of not being granted the favours I am so bold as to ask of you, I will tell you ways and means.'

I at first refused to hear of them, but was soon weak enough to beg him to tell me. These means, Monsieur, involved us meeting three times a week at the home of a certain Mme Berceil, a milliner in the rue des Arcis, for whose discretion and uprightness M. de — could vouch as much as if she were his mother.

'Since you are allowed to see your aunt who lives, as you have told me, quite near Madame Berceil, you will just have to pretend you are going to your aunt's, and indeed to pay her short visits, so that you can spend the rest of the time you might have devoted to her with the woman I have mentioned; if anyone asks your aunt, she will reply that she does indeed receive you on the days you go to see her – so you will merely have to keep an eye on how long you spend on your visits, though you can be sure nobody will ever pay any attention to this once you have gained people's confidence.'

I will not tell you, Monsieur, all the objections I made to M. de — to put him off this plan and show him all its drawbacks; what would be the point of describing my resistance, since in the end I yielded? I promised M. de — all that he wanted, and twenty louis that he gave Julie, unbeknownst to me, ensured that the girl was altogether won over to his cause, and from now on everything I did merely hastened my own downfall. To make this downfall all the more complete, and so that I could intoxicate myself for longer, and more at my leisure, on the sweet poison that was pouring onto my heart, I pretended to confide in my aunt that a young lady friend of mine (whom I had let into the secret so that she would not inadvertently betray me) had been so kind as to invite me three times a week into her box at the Théâtre-Français, that I did not dare tell this to my father in case he withheld his permission, but that I would say I was coming to see her, and I begged her to vouch for me. My aunt was initially rather hesitant, but could not resist my pleadings, and we decided that Julie would come to her house instead of me, and that on my way home from the theatre I would pick her up so that we could go home together. I hugged my aunt over and over again: in the fateful blindness of my passions, I thanked her for conniving in my destruction, and for opening the door to the madness that would bring me to the edge of the grave!

Finally, our meetings at the home of the Berceil woman began; her shop was magnificent, and she kept a very decent house; she herself was a woman of forty years or so, whom I thought I could trust completely. Alas! I trusted her all too much, as I did my lover too… False man! For now is the time to confess to you, Monsieur… The sixth time I saw him in that fateful house, he gained such power over me, he so completely overwhelmed me that he took advantage of my weakness and in his arms I became the idol of his passion and the victim of my own. Cruel pleasures, how many tears you have cost me already, and with how much remorse you will lacerate my soul until I breathe my last!

One year went by in this fateful illusion, Monsieur, and I had just reached my seventeenth year; every day my father spoke of finding me a husband, and you can guess how these remarks made me shudder, when a dreadful incident finally toppled me headlong into the eternal abyss. This was doubtless done, alas, with the permission of Providence, which decreed that a matter in which I was not at fault should be precisely the one that served to punish me for my real faults, so as to demonstrate that we never escape that Providence, that it follows those who go astray wherever they may be, and that the very event that we least suspect brings about, without our noticing it, the event by which Providence is avenged.

Monsieur de — had informed me, one day, that some essential business would prevent him from enjoying the pleasure of my company for the three whole hours we usually spent together, but that he would come a few minutes before the end of the time allotted, although, if only so as not to disturb our usual habits, I should still come and spend as much time as usual at the home of the Berceil woman. In fact, for an hour or two, I would still enjoy myself more with that shopkeeper and her girls than I would do if I stayed alone at my father's. I felt I could rely on this woman well enough not to have any objections to my lover's suggestion. So I promised that I would come, begging him not to keep me waiting too long. He assured me that he would complete his business as quickly as possible, and I arrived – on that day that was to be so dreadful for me!

Berceil met me at the entrance to her shop, but would not let me go up to her rooms as she usually did.

'Mademoiselle,' she said as soon as she saw me, 'I am delighted that Monsieur de — cannot be punctual this evening. I have something private to tell you that I dare not confide in him, something that requires us both to step outside right away, just for a moment – as we could not have done had he been here.'

'What is this all about, Madame?' I said, rather alarmed at these opening remarks.

'Nothing at all, Mademoiselle, nothing at all,' replied Berceil. 'I can tell you straightaway you have nothing to worry about, it is the simplest thing in the world; my mother has found out about your affair, and she is an old harridan, as inquisitive as a confessor; I try to keep on the right side of her just for her money. She absolutely refuses to let me receive you, and I dare not tell Monsieur de —; but here is my plan. I will take you right now to the house of one of my colleagues, a woman of my age, just as trustworthy as myself, and I will introduce you to her; if you like her, you will admit to Monsieur de — that I took you there, that she is an honest woman and that you find it a very good idea for your meetings with him to take place there; if you do not like her, which I feel most unlikely, then since we will have been there for just a few moments, you will refrain from telling him what we have done; then I will take it upon myself to inform him that I can no longer lend him my house, and you will both discuss what other means you can find of meeting.'

What this woman was telling me was so simple, the expression and manner she used so natural, my trust so entire and my innocence so total that I did not have the slightest difficulty in granting her what she asked. I merely regretted the fact that, as she said, she could no longer help us as she had; I expressed this regret in heartfelt tones, and we left. The house to which I was taken was in the same street, sixty or eighty paces away from Berceil's; it seemed not unattractive on the outside, with a carriage entrance, some fine casement windows overlooking the street, and an air of decency and cleanliness everywhere, and yet a secret voice seemed to be crying out in the depths of my heart, warning me that some strange event awaited me in this fateful house; I felt a sort of reluctance at every step I climbed, and everything seemed to be saying to me, 'Where are you going, unhappy woman? Fly from this place of perdition!…' Still, here we were; we entered a rather fine antechamber where we did not see anyone, and from there went into a salon whose door closed immediately behind us, as if someone had been hiding behind it… I shuddered, it was very dark in this salon, and you could barely see to find your way around; we had not taken three steps before I felt myself being seized by two women; then the door to a small room opened, in which I saw a man of around fifty between two other women who cried to those who had seized me, 'Strip her, strip her bare! Do not bring her here until she is completely naked!' Emerging from the daze I had fallen into when those women had laid hands on me, and seeing that any hope of escape depended more on my screams than on my fears, I proceeded to utter ear-piercing screams. Berceil did everything she could to calm me down.

'It will just take a minute, Mademoiselle,' she said. 'Just go along with it for now, I beg you, and you will earn fifty louis for me.'

'You hateful old harridan!' I retorted. 'Do not think you can traffic my honour like this! I will fling myself out of the windows if you do not get me out of here this very minute.'

'You would simply find yourself in a courtyard where you would soon be recaptured, my child,' said one of those rascally women, tearing off my clothes. 'So believe you me, it will all be over more quickly if you just play along…'

Oh Monsieur, spare me the rest of these horrible details! I was stripped bare in seconds, my cries were barbarously stifled, and I was dragged over to the vile man who, mocking my tears and making light of my resistance, was intent only on mastering the unhappy victim whose heart he was rending; two women continued to hold me down and deliver me to this monster; and though he was in a position to do whatever he wanted, he merely dowsed the flames of his criminal lust by impure kisses and caresses that did not entirely sully my honour…

They quickly helped me get dressed again, and handed me back to Berceil. I was stunned and dazed, overwhelmed by a kind of dark and bitter pain that froze my tears in the depths of my heart; I darted furious glances at that woman…

'Mademoiselle,' she said to me in the greatest dismay while we were still in the antechamber of that fateful house, 'I am aware of the full horror of what I have just done, but I beg you to forgive me… and to reflect, at least, before you yield to the idea of raising any hue and cry; if you reveal what has happened to Monsieur de —, however much you claim that you were forced into it, it is a kind of fault for which he will never forgive you, and you will have fallen out with the one man in the world with whom you need to stay on good terms, since the only way you can repair the honour that he has stolen is if you can persuade him to marry you. Now you may be sure that he will never do so if you tell him what has just happened.'

'Wretched woman! Why then have you plunged me into this pit of despair, why have you put me in a situation where either

I must deceive my lover, or else lose both my honour and him?'

'Hush, Madame, let us talk no more of what is done, time presses, let us think of what we need to do. If you say anything, you are doomed; if you do not breathe a word, my house will always be open to you, your secret will never be betrayed by anyone, and you remain on the best of terms with your lover; just see if the small satisfaction of vengeance (which I can always treat with utter scorn, since I know your secret and will always be able to stop Monsieur de — from harming me), yes, just see if the paltry pleasure of that vengeance will compensate for all the sorrows it brings in its wake…'

Realising what a vile woman I was dealing with, and fully persuaded by the force of her arguments, however abominable, I said to her, 'Let us go, Madame, let us go, do not leave me in this house any longer; I will not breathe a word, and you must do likewise; I will use your services since I could not dismiss you without revealing disgraceful events that I absolutely must conceal, but I will at least, in my heart of hearts, have the satisfaction of hating and despising you as you so thoroughly deserve.'

We returned to Berceil's house… Good heavens, great was my dismay when I was informed that M. de — had come, that he had been told that Madame had gone out on urgent business and that Mademoiselle had not yet arrived! At the same time one of the shop girls handed me a note he had scribbled down for me. It contained just these words:

I did not find you here, I imagine you were unable to come at the usual time, I will be unable to see you this evening, I cannot wait, I will see you the day after tomorrow without fail.

The note did not calm me in the slightest; it was written in a somewhat frigid style that seemed to augur no good… Not to wait for me, to show so little patience… All of this filled me with an agitation that I cannot describe; might he have realised what we were doing and followed us – and if he had done so, was I not dishonoured? Berceil, just as anxious as myself, questioned everyone, and was told that M. de — had arrived three minutes after we had gone out, that he had looked very worried, that he had immediately taken his leave and returned to write this note perhaps half an hour later. Now even more anxious, I sent out for a carriage… But can you believe, Monsieur, to what level of brazen impudence that old hussy dared to carry her vile plans?

'Mademoiselle,' she said, when she saw me leaving, 'never breathe a word of what has happened; I cannot urge this on you often enough, but if by any mischance you happen to quarrel with Monsieur de —, then believe you me, make the most of your freedom to court several other men; that is much better than taking one lover. I know that you are a respectable young woman, but you are young, and they doubtless give you very little money – and, being as pretty as you are, I will help you earn as much as you want… Come now, you are not the only woman in such a position, and there are many who strut around in all their finery who marry, as you too will be able to one day, counts or *marquis*, and who, either of their own free will or through the intervention of their governesses, have passed through our hands like you; we have men who are just the thing for little dolls of your kind, just as you have seen; they use a girl as if she were a rose, savouring her perfume but not withering her bloom. Farewell, my beauty, let us not get sulky, you can see perfectly well that I can still be of use to you.'

I threw a horror-stricken glance at this creature, and rushed out without replying; I picked up Julie at my aunt's house as usual, and returned home.

I had no way of communicating with M. de —. Since we met three times a week, we were not in the habit of writing, so I would have to wait until the time of our next assignation… What would he say to me? What would I reply? Would I cover up what had happened? If so, was I not running the greatest danger if what had happened came out? Would it not be wiser to tell him everything?… All these different possible lines of action kept me in an indescribable state of anxiety. Finally I resolved to follow Berceil's advice, and as I knew full well that it was in this woman's best interests to keep the secret, I decided to follow her example and say nothing… Good heavens, what use were all these schemes, since I was never to see my lover again, and the thunderbolt that was about to come crashing down on my head was already glowering wherever I looked!

My older brother asked me, the day after these events, why I was taking the liberty of going out by myself so many times a week, and at such hours of the day.

'I go to spend the evenings with my aunt,' I told him.

'That is not true, Émilie, you have not set foot there for a month.'

'Well, my dear brother,' I replied, trembling, 'I will confess everything to you: one of my friends whom you know well, Madame de Saint-Clair, is so kind as to take me three times a week to her box in the Théâtre-Français; I did not dare mention this, for fear that my father would disapprove, but my aunt is fully apprised of the fact.'

'So, you go to the theatre,' said my brother. 'You might have told me, I would have come with you, and it would all have been so much simpler… But to go there alone with a woman who is not in the least related to you and is almost as young as you are…'

'Come now, my friend,' said my other brother who had just come up as we were talking, 'Mademoiselle has her pleasures, we must not get in the way… she is looking for a husband, that is for sure, and they will come crowding round her once they see how she behaves…'

And both of them turned on their heels. This conversation filled me with alarm; however, since my older brother seemed quite persuaded by my story about the theatre box, I also imagined I had succeeded in deceiving him and that he would take the matter no further. In any case, even if both of them had had more to say about it, unless they had actually locked me up, no violence would have been great enough to prevent me going to the next meeting with my lover; it was now absolutely essential that I clear things up with him, and nothing in the world would have deprived me of the possibility of going to see him.

As far as my father was concerned, he was the same as ever; he idolised me, never suspected any of my misdemeanours, and never hindered me from doing anything. How cruel it is to have to deceive such parents! The remorse that arises in consequence sows thorns amid the pleasures that one purchases with betrayals of this kind! Fateful error, cruel passion – if you could but preserve from my mistakes those women who may chance to find themselves in the same situation as myself! And may the pains that my criminal pleasures cost me at least halt them on the brink of the abyss, if they ever learn of my sad and terrible story.

Finally, the fateful day arrived. I took Julie with me and slipped out in the usual way; I left her at my aunt's and hurried in my fiacre to Berceil's house. I climbed out... The silence and the darkness in which that house was enveloped immediately filled me with dread... Nobody whose face I recognised came to meet me; the only person to appear was an old woman whom I had never seen and of whom I was – alas! – to see all too much. She told me to remain in the room where I was, and M. de — (here she uttered his name) would come to me straightaway. A shudder of cold ran through my body, and I fell into an arm-chair without the strength to say a word; no sooner was I there than my two brothers presented themselves, holding pistols.

'Wretched woman!' exclaimed the elder of the two, 'so this is how you play us false! If you put up the least resistance, if you utter a single cry, you are dead. Follow us; we will teach you to betray both the family that you dishonour, and the lover to whom you have given yourself!'

At these words, I completely lost consciousness, and by the time I came round, I found myself in a carriage that seemed to be travelling very fast, between my two brothers and the old woman I have just mentioned, with my legs tied, and my hands bound in a handkerchief; my tears, held in up until now by the excess of my pain, now burst forth in abundance and for an hour I was in a state that, however great my guilt, would have softened the heart of anyone other than the two tormentors in whose hands I found myself. They did not talk me to on the way; I imitated their silence and remained sunk in my abjection. Finally, we arrived the next day, at eleven in the morning, at our destination: a place between Coucy and Noyon, a castle in the midst of the woods that belonged to my older brother. The carriage entered the courtyard; I was ordered to stay there until the horses and the servants had gone, then my older brother came to fetch me. 'Follow me,' he said brutally once he had untied me... I obeyed, trembling... God, how horrified I was when I discovered the dismal retreat that was to serve as my dwelling! It was a low-ceilinged room, dark, damp and gloomy, with iron bars on every side and drawing just a little wan light through a single window that overlooked a wide ditch filled with water.

'This is your abode, Mademoiselle,' said my brothers. 'A girl who dishonours her family is bound to find it a suitable place… Your food will be in proportion to the rest of the treatment; this is what you will be given,' they continued, showing me a hunk of bread of the kind given to animals, 'and since we do not wish to make you suffer for long, while on the other hand we want to deprive you of all means of getting out of here, these two women' (and here they pointed to the old woman and another similar one whom we had seen in the castle) 'will be given the task of bleeding both your arms just as many times per week as you went to see Monsieur de — at the house of Berceil; gradually – at least this is what we hope – this treatment will bring you to the grave, and we will only fully be satisfied when we learn that the family has been rid of a monster such as you.'

With these words, he ordered those women to seize me, and in front of them, those villains – forgive me for the expression, Monsieur – in front of them… the cruel men bled both of my arms at once and only halted this cruel treatment when they saw that I had lost consciousness… When I came round, I found them congratulating themselves on their barbarous behaviour, and as if they had wanted every blow to fall on me simultaneously, as if they had delighted in rending my heart at the same instant as they were shedding my blood, the older pulled a letter from his pocket, and presented it to me, saying, 'Read this, Mademoiselle, read this, and discover to whom you owe your misfortunes…'

I opened it, trembling, and my eyes hardly had the strength to recognise that fateful handwriting. Great God… it was my lover himself, it was he who had betrayed me; this was the content of this cruel letter, and its words are still imprinted on my heart in letters of blood.

I have been foolish enough to love your sister, Monsieur, and imprudent enough to dishonour her; I planned to make reparations for everything; gnawed by remorse, I was about to fall at your father's feet, confess my guilt and ask for his daughter in marriage; I would have been sure of my own father's agreement, and my background meant I would have made a suitable member of your family. Just as I had decided on this course of action… my eyes, my own eyes convinced me that I was dealing with nothing more than a common whore who, under the pretext of lovers' meetings that were motivated by a feeling both honest and pure, made so bold as to satisfy the vile desires of the most debauched of men. So do not expect any reparation from me now, Monsieur, as I no longer owe you any; to you I owe nothing but silence and distance, and to her the most inviolable hatred and the most unswerving contempt. I am sending you the address of the house where your sister went to wallow in corruption, Monsieur, so that you may find out whether I am misleading you.

Hardly had I read these fateful words than I relapsed into the most dreadful state… 'No,' I said to myself, tearing out my hair, 'no, cruel man, you never loved me; if the slightest feeling ever warmed your heart, would you have condemned me without giving me a hearing, would you have supposed me to be guilty of such a crime, when you were the man I adored?… Traitor! To think that it is your hand that is delivering me to my captors, your hand that is pushing me into the arms of tormentors who will make me die a little more, piecemeal, day by day… die without being justified by you… die despised by the only man I adore, when I have never deliberately offended him, when I have never been anything other than a dupe and a victim, ah no, no, this situation is too cruel, I do not have the strength to tolerate it!' And flinging myself in tears at the feet of my brothers, I begged them to hear me, or to stop letting my blood drain away drop by drop and allow me to die upon the instant.

They condescended to hear me out and I told them my story, but they were intent on destroying me and refused to believe me. Their treatment of me simply became even harsher: they heaped insults upon me and ordered the two women to carry out their orders to the letter, on pain of death; then they left me, coldly assuring me that they hoped they would never see me again.

As soon as they were gone, my two prison keepers left me with bread and water and locked me in, but at least I was alone; I could abandon myself to the excess of my despair, and I found myself feeling less wretched. At first, my despair drove me to untie the bandages on my arms, and to let myself die by allowing the rest of my blood to flow out. But the horrid idea of ceasing to live without being justified in the eyes of my lover tore so violently at my heart that I simply could not bring myself to do so; a little calm soon brings back hope… Hope, that consolatory feeling that always arises in the midst of our pains, that divine gift that nature grants us to counterbalance or soften them… 'No,' I told myself, 'I will not die without seeing him, that must be the sole object for which I work, with that end alone I must busy myself; if he persists in believing me to be guilty, then it will be time to die, and indeed I will do so without a qualm, since it is impossible for life to hold any delight for me once I have lost his love.'

Once I had reached this decision, I resolved to neglect none of the means that might enable me to escape from this odious cell. I had been consoling myself with this thought for four days when my two jailors reappeared to replenish my provisions and at the same time deprive me of what little strength they gave me; once again they bled me from both my arms, and left me lying motionless in bed; on the eighth day they reappeared, and as I flung myself at their feet to beg for mercy, they bled me from just one arm. Two whole months went by like this, during which I was constantly bled from each arm alternately, every four days. The strength of my temperament sustained me, my age, the excessive desire I had to escape from this terrible situation, the amount of bread that I ate to recover from my exhaustion and to be able to carry out my plans… All went as I had hoped, and around the beginning of the third month, having been fortunate enough to break through one of the walls and to slip through this hole into the next room, whose door was unlocked, and to make my escape from the castle, I was struggling to make my way on foot, as best I could, to the Paris road, when my strength completely abandoned me at the place you found me, and you, Monsieur, granted me the generous succour for which my sincere gratitude will repay you as much as is in my power. I beg you to continue to bestow it on me, so that you will bring me safely to my father, who has certainly been deceived and who will never be so barbarous as to condemn me without allowing me to prove my innocence to him. I will convince him that I have been weak, but he will soon see that I have not been as guilty as appearances seem to prove, and by your help, Monsieur, you will not only have restored to life a wretched creature who will never cease to thank you for so doing, but you will also have restored the honour of a family that believes it has been robbed of it.

'Mademoiselle,' said the Count de Luxeuil after paying Émilie's story all the attention of which he was capable, 'it is difficult to see and hear you without having one's sympathies for you aroused to the full; doubtless you have not been as guilty as people seem to think, but there is in your behaviour a certain imprudence that you must find very difficult to conceal from yourself.'

'Oh, Monsieur!'

'Listen to me, Mademoiselle, I beg you, listen to the man who more than anyone else in the world desires to be of service to you. The behaviour of your lover is dreadful; not only is it unjust, since he should have taken pains to clarify the situation and to come and see you, but it is, indeed, cruel; if a man becomes so prejudiced against a woman as to desire to have nothing further to do with her, he can in that case abandon her, but he does not denounce her to her family, he does not dishonour her, he does not vilely abandon her to those who will destroy her, he does not urge them on to avenge them-selves… So I utterly condemn the behaviour of the man with whom you were in love… But your brothers' actions are much more abhorrent, being hateful in every respect, and only torturers can behave in such a way. Misdemeanours of this kind do not deserve such punishments: binding people in chains has never been of the slightest good; you may withhold speech from the guilty, but you do not deprive them of their blood or of their freedom; those odious measures dishonour those who employ them much more than they do their victims, whose hatred they justly arouse; in such cases, for all the commotion one has caused, no reparation for the crime has been exacted. However dear the virtue of a sister may be to us, her life must be even more precious in our eyes; honour can be restored, but not the blood that has been shed. So this behaviour is so horrible that it would most assuredly be punished if one laid a complaint with the authorities, but these measures would merely mimic those of your persecutors, and would bring to the public attention what we ought to conceal; so they are not the measures to which we should resort. So I will help you best by adopting a quite different course of action, Mademoiselle; still, I warn you that I can do so only on the following conditions: the first is that you will not fail to give me in writing the addresses of your father, your aunt, Madame Berceil, and the man to whom Berceil took you, and the second, Mademoiselle, is that you will without demur give me the name of the man who has aroused your affections. This clause is so essential that I will not hide from you the fact that it is altogether impossible for me to help you in any way whatsoever if you persist in withholding from me the name I require from you.'

Émilie, in perplexity, started fulfilling the first condition to the letter, and when she had given the Count the addresses he had asked for, she added, blushing, 'So you require me, Monsieur, to give you the name of my seducer.'

'Absolutely, Mademoiselle, I can do nothing without it.'

'Very well, Monsieur… he is the Marquis de Luxeuil…'

'The Marquis de Luxeuil!' cried the Count, unable to disguise his feelings on hearing that the man in question was his son. 'So *he* is the perpetrator of the deed?' And then, mastering his emotion: 'He will pay for it, Mademoiselle… He will pay for it and you will be avenged… You have my word for it. Farewell.'

The surprise and consternation into which Émilie's last confession had just thrown the Count de Luxeuil took that unfortunate woman aback; she feared she had been indiscreet, and yet the words uttered by the Count as he left reassured her, and without understanding in the least how all these facts were related (something she could not piece together), and since she did not know where she was, she resolved to wait patiently for her benefactor's actions to bear fruit, and the constant care with which she was surrounded while he carried out his task managed finally to calm her and to convince her that her happiness was their sole aim.

She had every right to feel fully reassured when, on the fourth day after she had given him her account of events, she saw the Count enter her room, leading the Marquis de Luxeuil in by the hand.

'Mademoiselle,' said the Count, 'I bring you both the author of your misfortunes and the man who has come to make up for them by begging you on his knees not to refuse him your hand in marriage.'

At these words, the Marquis flung himself at the feet of the woman he adored, but the surprise had been too great for Émilie; not strong enough to bear the shock, she had fainted in the arms of her servant woman, but with the help of the latter she had soon recovered the use of her senses and found herself in the arms of her lover.

'Cruel man,' she told him, shedding floods of tears, 'what sorrow and pain you have caused the woman you loved! Could you believe her capable of the infamy of which you dared to suspect her? Émilie loves you, and while she could be the victim of her own weakness and of the villainy of others, she could never be unfaithful.'

'Ah, how I adore you!' exclaimed the Marquis. 'Forgive an attack of horrible jealousy that was based on deceptive appearances, as we are now both fully convinced – but alas, were not those appearances unfortunately against you?'

'You should have had enough esteem for me, Luxeuil, and not believed that I could ever be a woman to betray you; you should have paid less attention to your despair than to the feelings that I fondly imagined I had aroused in you. May this be a lesson to my sex: it is almost always by loving too much... almost always by giving ourselves too quickly that we lose the esteem of our lovers... Ah Luxeuil, you would have loved me better if I had loved you less quickly; you have punished me for my weakness, and what should have strengthened your love made you doubt mine.'

'Let bygones be bygones for both of you,' interrupted the Count; 'Luxeuil, your behaviour was reprehensible and if you had not immediately offered to make up for it, if I had not seen clearly that you were resolved in your heart to do so, I would have banished you forever from my sight. When a man loves a woman, as our old troubadours used to say, even if he has heard or seen something that puts his beloved in a bad light, he should believe neither his ears nor his eyes, he should listen to his heart alone.* Mademoiselle, I await your full recovery with impatience,' pursued the Count, turning to Émilie. 'I can take you back to your parents only when you are the bride of my son, and I dare to hope that they will not refuse to see our two families linked in compensation for your misfortunes; if they do not do so, I offer you my house, Mademoiselle; your wedding will be celebrated there, and until my dying breath I will never cease to consider you as a

* It was the troubadours of Provence who said this, not the Picards. [Sade's note.]

cherished daughter-in-law by whom I will always be honoured, whether her marriage meets or does not meet with approval.' Luxeuil flung his arms round his father, Mlle de Tourville burst into tears as she pressed her benefactor's hands, and she was left alone for a few hours to recover from a scene that, if prolonged any further, would have hindered the recovery that was desired so ardently on both sides.

Finally, two weeks after her return to Paris, Mlle de Tourville was in a fit state to get up and climb into a carriage; the Count had her clothed in a white dress that perfectly matched the innocence of her heart; nothing was neglected that might intensify her already dazzling allure, made even more attractive by the slight pallor and debility from which she was still suffering. The Count, Luxeuil and herself drove to the home of the Président de Tourville, who knew nothing and was taken completely by surprise when he saw his daughter entering. He was with his two sons, whose brows furrowed with anger and rage at this unexpected sight; they knew their sister had escaped, but they thought she had died in the depths of the forest, and – as can be seen – had consoled themselves for her loss as easily as anything.

'Monsieur,' said the Count, presenting Émilie to her father, 'here is the very picture of innocence that I bring to kneel at your feet' – whereupon Émilie threw herself before him… 'I implore you to have mercy on her, Monsieur,' continued the Count, 'and I would be the last person to ask this of you if I were not certain that she deserved it; furthermore, Monsieur,' he continued quickly, 'the best proof I can give you of the deep respect in which I hold your daughter is that I am asking you for her hand in marriage on behalf of my son. We are both of equal social standing, Monsieur, our families can be joined; were there any disparity in wealth on my side,

I would sell all I own to ensure my son had a fortune worthy of being offered to your daughter. The decision is yours, Monsieur, and allow me not to leave you before you have given me your word.'

The old Président de Tourville, who had always adored his dear Émilie, was goodness and kindness in person; indeed, his excellent character meant that he had not discharged his legal duties for over twenty years. Shedding tears on the breast of his dear child, the old President replied to the Count that he was only too happy at this choice, that his only anxiety was that Émilie was not worthy; whereupon the Marquis de Luxeuil in turn fell to his knees before the President, begging him to forgive him his errors and give him an opportunity to make up for them. Promises were exchanged, plans were laid, calm was restored on both sides; only the brothers of our lovely heroine refused to share the general joy and thrust her back when she stepped forward to embrace them; the Count, furious at this behaviour, tried to stop one of them as he made to leave the room. Monsieur de Tourville exclaimed to the Count, 'Leave them, Monsieur, leave them, they most dreadfully deceived me; if this dear child had been as guilty as they made out to me, would you agree to give her in marriage to your son? They darkened the happiness of my days by depriving me of my dear Émilie… let them go…'

And those wretches left, raging and cursing. Then the Count told M. de Tourville of all the horrible crimes they had committed and of the misdemeanours of which his daughter was truly guilty; the President could find little proportion between her faults and the indignity of her punishment, and swore that he would never see his sons again. The Count calmed him down, and made him promise that he would wipe their deeds from his memory. A week later, the wedding was celebrated without the brothers wishing to attend; they were not missed, but rather viewed with contempt; M. de Tourville contented himself with recommending they keep the greatest silence on pain of being locked up in their turn, and they did keep silence – though they still could not refrain from puffing up with pride at their vile actions and condemning their father's indulgence; and all those who learned of this unhappy sequence of events cried out in dismay at the atrocious details that characterised them, 'Good heavens! Such, then, are the horrors that those meddlers who assume responsibility for punishing the crimes of others tacitly allow themselves! One has every right to conclude that vile deeds of this kind are the preserve of those crazed and inept henchmen of blind Themis whose upbringing is over-severe to the point of stupidity, who learn from earliest childhood to turn a deaf ear to the cries of misfortune, who are stained with blood from the cradle onwards, who condemn everything and indulge in everything, imagining that the only way to cover up their private vices and their public injustices is to affect a rigid and unbending manner that, making them resemble geese on the outside and tigers within, has as its sole aim, while sullying them with every crime, the purpose of deceiving gullible fools and leading the wise man to hate their odious principles, their bloodthirsty laws, and their contemptible selves.'

NOTES

1. Flora was the Roman goddess of flowers, youth and spring; in Greek mythology, the Graces were three goddesses (Aglaia, Euphrosyne and Thalia) who were daughters of Zeus and Hera and the personifications of pleasure, charm and beauty.

2. For the sake of simplicity the French word *Président* has been translated 'President', though the *Président* of a *Parlement* was something like the presiding judge of a high judicial court. There were *parlements* in Paris and all of the provinces.

3. In this sketch, Sade satirises the speech of the inhabitants of Provence, who rolled (and still do) their 'r's like characters from the *commedia dell'arte*, and more generally like Italians. Fontanis tends to be most *provençal* when uttering oaths.

4. Themis was the ancient goddess of Justice, and the magistrates of Provence are here seen as her temple.

5. A *remontrance* could be a complaint brought to the king, or one of various other kinds of legal admonition.

6. St Paul claimed to have been swept up to the third heaven: see 2 Corinthians 12:2–4.

7. French writers on jurisprudence of the seventeenth and sixteenth centuries respectively.

8. Ostrogothic presumably because the word makes him sound ugly (and the Ostrogoths settled in Italy and Provence). Justinian I, the Emperor of Byzantium, had the codification of law known as the *Digest* drawn up; he was responsible for the destruction of the Ostrogoth kingdom (AD 535–55).

9. An *hôtel* could be either a hotel or, especially in seventeenth- and eighteenth-century usage, the private residence of a member of the upper classes. The Hôtel de Danemark (not to be confused with the present-day Hôtel Danemark in the rue Vavin, nearby) was in the rue Jacob, in the Latin Quarter of Paris: it was here that, on 13th February 1776, Sade was arrested by Inspector Marais and taken to the fortress prison at Vincennes.

10. This fair, renowned throughout Europe, held in the Saint-Germain area of Paris, went back to 1176.

11. Nicolet's *Gaîté* was a well-known boulevard theatre, as was Audinot's *Ambigu Comique*.

12. The Roman poet Horace enjoined the use of these scents.

13. Lawyers (see note 4).

14. 'Philosophy' presumably alludes here to the rational, enlightened attitudes of the *philosophes* such as Diderot and Voltaire who criticised the abuses (including legal over-severity and corruption) of the *ancien régime*.

15. Law court, as in ancient Athens.

16. The Sibyl of Cumae, near Naples, lived in a cave with a hundred mouths, and like all sibyls was famed for the obscurity of her oracular utterances.

17. These 'machines' are the contrivances that will be used to enact the President's humiliation.

18. The President actually says, '*Et tout aque par ici, et tout aque par ila*,' a French-Provençal phrase: the word *aque* means *avec* – 'with'.

19. The Roman god of medicine.

20. The marriage, although sacramentally celebrated at Saint-Sulpice, has not yet been consummated: so sometimes she is Fontanis's 'bride', sometimes still his betrothed.

21. Actually, he says *Péchaire!*, a common Provençal oath.

22. There may be a pun here: '*on n'a pas toujours la foire*': 'one does not always have *la foire*', where *foire* can mean 'fair' (as in the Saint-Germain fair) but also 'diarrhoea'.

23. The sanctuary of Aesculapius (in Greek, Asklepios) at Epidauros was the most famous centre of healing in the ancient world.

24. The ancient, possibly legendary, law-giver of Sparta.

25. See Leviticus 11:7, where God tells Moses (and Aaron), 'And the pig, though it has a split hoof completely divided, does not chew the cud; it is unclean for you.'

26. Here and on other occasions Sade writes *frère* ('brother') when 'brother-in-law' is meant.

27. Comus was the Greek god of feasting and revelry (especially at night).

28. Tenaros, now Matapan, a cape on the southernmost point of the Peloponnese; its cave was reputed by the Ancients to be the home of Hades.

29. Abnormal excitability.

30. A centre of medical learning.

31. These towns in Provence were centres of the Albigensian religion, savagely crushed by the Catholic barons of northern France with the help of the Inquisition.

32. Surgeon. The church of Saint-Côme used to stand in the Latin Quarter, near what is now the corner between the rue Monsieur-le-Prince and the Boulevard Saint-Michel; in the Middle Ages, a circle of surgeons would gather in a room near the burial ground adjacent, and came to be known as the 'confraternity of Saint-Côme'.

33. Another circumlocution for 'doctor'.

34. Presumably the rope is one hanging in mid-air and used to guide the small ferry across the river.

35. An allusion to the Marseilles affair discussed in the introduction.

36. i.e. lawyers and priests respectively.

37. Pantaloon was a character in the *commedia dell'arte*, represented as an old man wearing pantaloons.

38. Possibly a reference to the occasional charge of cowardice levelled against Caesar. 'His coward lips did from their colour fly,' says Cassius of one such occasion in Shakespeare's *Julius Caesar* (I.ii.124).

39. Sade, unusually censoring his own text, gives just the initial 'p' of *putain* or 'whore': this was common practice in 'respectable' French prose well into the twentieth century.

40. Jean Calas, a Calvinist of Toulouse, was found guilty of killing his son for wishing to convert to Catholicism, and executed in 1762. Voltaire laboured – successfully – to have him posthumously rehabilitated.

41. A slightly obscure reference, since the reign of Charles VII (1422–61) was a time of notable French success in the Hundred Years War; he was the king crowned at Reims thanks to the efforts of Joan of Arc.

42. These details – including the date – fit the *affaire de Marseille*, though the text seems to include a reference to the *affaire d'Arcueil* also.

43. Phryne, the celebrated courtesan of ancient Greece, and the mistress and model of the sculptor Praxiteles, was brought before the Athenian court accused of capital offences, but at her trial she was defended by Hyperides; he pulled the garment from her breasts in a successful attempt to gain the sympathy of the audience.

44. i.e. your lawyer – Demosthenes was one of the most famous Athenian orators.

45. This may again refer to Sade's own career, as he had served his king successfully as a soldier in the Seven Years War, and had been exiled briefly for the Arcueil affair (mentioned in the introduction), returning to Paris in 1769.

46. A town and former capital of Lower Burma.

47. The Order of Saint-Louis was a military order of chivalry founded by King Louis XIV, and finally abolished in 1830.

48. Paphos on Cyprus was the legendary birthplace of the goddess of love, Aphrodite.

49. Under the French monarchy, the right of levying taxes was farmed out to local people in return for a cash payment. These were called farmers general.

50. Probably meaning Venus (Mlle de Téroze) over the goat (her husband, horned like a goat, i.e. a cuckold).

51. Agnes is the patron saint of innocence.

52. The *parlement* of Aix encouraged the local people to rebel against taxation during the minority of Louis XIV.

53. The army of Charles V invaded France during the reign of François I, and in August 1524 the Constable of Bourbon easily captured Aix.

54. This was the Catholic League, created in 1584 to defend the rights of Catholics against Protestants during the wars of religion.

55. The *lettre de cachet* was one of the most resented abuses of the *ancien régime*: a letter signed and sealed by the king could often enforce decisions against which no appeal was possible. Sade himself was served a *lettre de cachet* at the behest of his mother-in-law. The sense here is that obtaining a royal sentence of imprisonment is preferable for Fontanis to being forced into exile.

56. The 'philosopher' may be Sade himself, who used these words in other works.

BIOGRAPHICAL NOTE

Donatien-Alphonse-François de Sade was born in Paris in 1740. His mother, a lady-in-waiting at the Condé palace, arranged for her son to become a playmate to the infant Prince de Condé. It was not long, however, before de Sade had insulted the young prince, and was sent away to live with his uncle, the Abbé de Sade, a man of notorious sexual deviance.

In 1754 de Sade entered military service and later fought in the Seven Years War, an experience he recounted in his diaries. In spite of his marriage to Renée-Pélagie de Montreuil in 1763, his debauched lifestyle continued, and in that year he was imprisoned for posing a 'moral threat to prostitutes'. Similar arrests followed. Chief among his critics was his mother-in-law who had never forgiven him for his seduction of her younger daughter, a novice. In 1772 de Sade was sentenced to death for 'an unnatural crime', but he managed to flee to Italy with his valet.

He eventually returned to France, but his sexual crimes continued. He was once more imprisoned in 1777, and was transferred to the Bastille in 1784. It was here that he penned *The 120 Days of Sodom* and *The Misfortunes of Virtue*.

De Sade somehow managed to survive the French Revolution, but in 1801 he was again arrested and later confined to an asylum. Here, he kept up his diaries and also staged various plays, often in the presence of Mme Quesnet, his long-term lover. Following his death in 1814, his eldest son burnt his remaining manuscripts.

Andrew Brown studied at the University of Cambridge, where he taught French for many years. He now works as a freelance teacher and translator. He is the author of *Roland Barthes: The*

Figures of Writing (OUP, 1993), and his translations include *Memoirs of a Madman* by Gustave Flaubert, *For a Night of Love* by Emile Zola, *The Jinx* by Théophile Gautier, *Mademoiselle de Scudéri* by E.T.A. Hoffmann, *Theseus* by André Gide, *Incest* by Marquis de Sade, *The Ghost-seer* by Friedrich von Schiller, *Colonel Chabert* by Honoré de Balzac, *Memoirs of an Egotist* by Stendhal, *Butterball* by Guy de Maupassant and *With the Flow* by Joris-Karl Huysmans, all published by Hesperus Press.

HESPERUS PRESS CLASSICS

Hesperus Press, as suggested by the Latin motto, is committed to bringing near what is far – far both in space and time. Works written by the greatest authors, and unjustly neglected or simply little known in the English-speaking world, are made accessible through new translations and a completely fresh editorial approach. Through these classic works, the reader is introduced to the greatest writers from all times and all cultures.

For more information on Hesperus Press, please visit our website: **www.hesperuspress.com**

ET REMOTISSIMA PROPE

SELECTED TITLES FROM HESPERUS PRESS

Author	Title	Foreword writer
Pietro Aretino	*The School of Whoredom*	Paul Bailey
Pietro Aretino	*The Secret Life of Nuns*	
Jane Austen	*Lesley Castle*	Zoë Heller
Jane Austen	*Love and Friendship*	Fay Weldon
Honoré de Balzac	*Colonel Chabert*	A.N. Wilson
Charles Baudelaire	*On Wine and Hashish*	Margaret Drabble
Giovanni Boccaccio	*Life of Dante*	A.N. Wilson
Charlotte Brontë	*The Spell*	
Emily Brontë	*Poems of Solitude*	Helen Dunmore
Mikhail Bulgakov	*Fatal Eggs*	Doris Lessing
Mikhail Bulgakov	*The Heart of a Dog*	A.S. Byatt
Giacomo Casanova	*The Duel*	Tim Parks
Miguel de Cervantes	*The Dialogue of the Dogs*	Ben Okri
Geoffrey Chaucer	*The Parliament of Birds*	
Anton Chekhov	*The Story of a Nobody*	Louis de Bernières
Anton Chekhov	*Three Years*	William Fiennes
Wilkie Collins	*The Frozen Deep*	
Joseph Conrad	*Heart of Darkness*	A.N. Wilson
Joseph Conrad	*The Return*	Colm Tóibín
Gabriele D'Annunzio	*The Book of the Virgins*	Tim Parks
Dante Alighieri	*The Divine Comedy: Inferno*	
Dante Alighieri	*New Life*	Louis de Bernières
Daniel Defoe	*The King of Pirates*	Peter Ackroyd
Marquis de Sade	*Incest*	Janet Street-Porter
Charles Dickens	*The Haunted House*	Peter Ackroyd
Charles Dickens	*A House to Let*	
Fyodor Dostoevsky	*The Double*	Jeremy Dyson
Fyodor Dostoevsky	*Poor People*	Charlotte Hobson
Alexandre Dumas	*One Thousand and One Ghosts*	

Sándor Petőfi	*John the Valiant*	George Szirtes
Francis Petrarch	*My Secret Book*	Germaine Greer
Luigi Pirandello	*Loveless Love*	
Edgar Allan Poe	*Eureka*	Sir Patrick Moore
Alexander Pope	*The Rape of the Lock and A Key to the Lock*	Peter Ackroyd
Antoine-François Prévost	*Manon Lescaut*	Germaine Greer
Marcel Proust	*Pleasures and Days*	A.N. Wilson
Alexander Pushkin	*Dubrovsky*	Patrick Neate
Alexander Pushkin	*Ruslan and Lyudmila*	Colm Tóibín
François Rabelais	*Pantagruel*	Paul Bailey
François Rabelais	*Gargantua*	Paul Bailey
Christina Rossetti	*Commonplace*	Andrew Motion
George Sand	*The Devil's Pool*	Victoria Glendinning
Jean-Paul Sartre	*The Wall*	Justin Cartwright
Friedrich von Schiller	*The Ghost-seer*	Martin Jarvis
Mary Shelley	*Transformation*	
Percy Bysshe Shelley	*Zastrozzi*	Germaine Greer
Stendhal	*Memoirs of an Egotist*	Doris Lessing
Robert Louis Stevenson	*Dr Jekyll and Mr Hyde*	Helen Dunmore
Theodor Storm	*The Lake of the Bees*	Alan Sillitoe
Leo Tolstoy	*The Death of Ivan Ilych*	
Leo Tolstoy	*Hadji Murat*	Colm Tóibín
Ivan Turgenev	*Faust*	Simon Callow
Mark Twain	*The Diary of Adam and Eve*	John Updike
Mark Twain	*Tom Sawyer, Detective*	
Oscar Wilde	*The Portrait of Mr W.H.*	Peter Ackroyd
Virginia Woolf	*Carlyle's House and Other Sketches*	Doris Lessing
Virginia Woolf	*Monday or Tuesday*	Scarlett Thomas
Emile Zola	*For a Night of Love*	A.N. Wilson